Angel

The Dykemaster

THEODOR STORM (1817-88) was born in Husum, a small coastal town in the Duchy of Schleswig, then under Danish rule, where he established himself as a lawyer. Exiled after the unsuccessful rising of 1848, he entered the Prussian judiciary. During the rising of 1863/4 he was popularly elected *in absentia* to the esteemed post of *Landvogt* (combining judicial and police powers), and returned to Husum. After Prussia's annexation of Schleswig-Holstein in 1867, to which he remained bitterly opposed, he settled for the modest post of *Amtsrichter* (district court judge).

In 1846 he married his cousin, Constanze Esmarch, but soon afterwards fell in love with Dorothea Jensen, the daughter of a Husum senator, whom, after Constanze's death in 1865, he eventually married. His second marriage was initially dominated by depression, both his own and his wife's. Severe difficulties with his three sons dogged him to the end of his life.

Storm began his literary career as a lyric poet. His early Novelle *Immensee* (1849), integrating lyric verse and narrative, was an immediate success, albeit misunderstood by its public. In all Storm wrote over fifty Novellen. He evolved a sophisticated narrative technique of conflicting perspectives, enabling him to draw his readers into sharing his critical attitudes to contemporary social norms. *Der Schimmelreiter* (1888), written while he was terminally ill, is his masterpiece.

The translator: DENIS JACKSON is a freelance translator, with a lifelong association with German language and culture. He has a detailed first-hand knowledge of the region in which Storm lived and wrote.

DAVID A. JACKSON, MA, DPHIL(Oxon.), contributor of the Afterword, is a Senior Lecturer in German Literature at the University of Wales College of Cardiff, and the author of *Theodor Storm: The Life and Works of a Democratic Humanitarian* (Oxford, 1992).

THEODOR STORM

The Dykemaster

(Der Schimmelreiter)

Translated with notes by
DENIS JACKSON

Afterword by David A. Jackson

ANGEL BOOKS
London

This translation is dedicated to the people of
North Friesland whose story it is and to whom
it belongs; to their indomitable spirit
in the face of constant danger
from the North Sea

First published in 1996 by
Angel Books, 3 Kelross Road, London N5 2QS
1 3 5 7 9 10 8 6 4 2

British Library Cataloguing in Publication Data:
A catalogue record for this book is available
from the British Library

ISBN 0 946162 54 9 pbk

This book is printed on Permanent Paper conforming to the British
Library recommendations and to the full American standard

The Publisher makes grateful acknowledgement to Inter Nationes,
Bonn for a grant towards translation costs

Typeset in Great Britain by
Metropress (Type) Ltd, Wellingborough, Northants
Printed and bound by
Woolnough Bookbinding Ltd, Irthlingborough, Northants

Contents

Translator's Preface

It is some years since the last English translation of Theodor Storm's *Der Schimmelreiter* appeared. I find that I am not alone in my view that earlier translations do not convince the reader that this work is one of the supreme achievements of German fiction. Earlier translators, however, did not have the benefit of a number of authoritative new editions and critical studies that have substantially advanced understanding of Storm's writing and provide today's translator with invaluable assistance. To win this dramatic tale its overdue place among the classics of European literature available in English has therefore been my aim in a long, difficult, but highly rewarding task.

The old Friesian saying that God created the sea but the Friesians the land could well serve as an epigraph to this work: its style and tone reflect the shifting moods of the sea and landscape, and its poetry the natural sounds and colours of marshland life. To even begin to provide a true translation of such a work demands not only a knowledge of the language of the author's time, but also an understanding of the North Friesian environment and its people; for without this, much of what the author writes of, with such skill and artistry, would be lost to the reader.

My travels and researches took me not only to the tall windswept dykes of North Friesland on the west coast of Schleswig-Holstein, to its lonely marshes and the limitless solitude of the North Sea tidal flats, the Wattenmeer, but also to the dykes along the Vistula in the north of Poland, to the original source of the story. All these journeys and inquiries made me acutely aware of the importance of these dykes to the North Friesian people whose daily lives depend upon them for protection, and of their constant fear of 'the wild North Sea' (*der blanke Hans*) and their eternal struggle against its terrifying and destructive power. This fear underlies the entire text, at one point in which the sea is perceived as a predatory animal that gnaws and bites at the dyke, and in another, in the mind of a child, speaks, has legs and can step over it to devour mankind. It is for this reason that I have translated Storm's title *Der Schimmelreiter,* meaning 'The Rider on the White Horse', or more properly 'The Rider on the Grey', as *The Dykemaster*. Not only has this the same firm conciseness as the German, but it also directly conveys to the English reader the theme and focal point of this tale which, in Storm's words, 'takes place somewhere behind the dykes in the North Friesian marshes'.

Storm was a man of his region, of the town of Husum on the flat North Friesian coast; a man of its heathland, dykes, marsh and polders. He was a meticulously keen observer and recorder of its changing seasons, its abundant wild life, its rich flora and fauna and its people. Nature and poetry were one to him and he expressed the view towards the end of his life that only those who had a close affinity with nature could understand the 'poetry of the heath and moorland, the coast, and the deathly quiet of its meadows behind the dykes'. He was first and foremost a poet, and his poetry not only reflected his deep affinity with the coastal region of his homeland but also greatly influenced his prose; as he wrote later in life to a close friend: 'My craft of fiction grew out of my lyric verse'. His words are chosen as much for their sounds as for their meanings, and his scenes are created with a breathtaking simplicity and precision in which no important detail is ever excluded. His dialogue, too, is sparse yet it fully conveys the essentials of his characters and what they are saying within their social environment. To render such economy and poetry in English has frequently been an impossible task. I have made, however, every effort to maintain the swiftness of Storm's language and the momentum of his style, and in particular to preserve in the text, supported by the end-notes, the fine details of Friesian life and culture that contribute so much to the impact of this work in which the local level is raised to universal significance.

The title of *Deichgraf* (Dykegrave, or Dykemaster in the present translation) is no longer in use in North Friesland; only the post of *Oberdeichgraf* (Chief Dykemaster) remains today. The planning and maintenance of the main sea defences, because of the significant costs involved, are now the responsibility of the state and not the local community. The Chief Dykemaster's present responsibilities rest with the second line of defence, the inner dykes, and the drainage of the marshland. But like the dykemaster of the Novelle, he is still required to provide a watch (*Deichgänger*) on the sea dyke during a storm, and as it was for former dykemasters, his post is also an elected one from within the polder communities affected. It is no sinecure and still carries many of the burdens Storm depicts. 'It's a responsible office, having to protect the community against the Lord God's sea,' says Storm's dykemaster, Hauke Haien; a statement as true today as it was in Storm's time and earlier.

The text I have used is that of the four-volume collected edition *Theodor Storm: Sämtliche Werke*, edited by Karl Ernst Laage and Dieter Lohmeier (Deutscher Klassiker Verlag, Frankfurt am Main, 1988); volume 3, *Novellen 1881-1888*, pp. 634-756, edited by Karl Ernst Laage. Reference has also been made to *Theodor Storm. Der Schimmelreiter. Sylter Novelle*, edited by Karl Ernst Laage (Westholsteinische Verlagsanstalt Boyens & Co., Heide, in conjunction with the Theodor-Storm-Gesellschaft, 1993).

Acknowledgements

To the President of the Theodor-Storm-Gesellschaft in Husum, Professor Dr Karl Ernst Laage, I am most indebted for his kind assistance throughout this project in supplying valuable advice and providing me with access to the Society's *Schimmelreiter* archives; also for his permission for the reproduction of detail of Alexander Eckener's oil painting *Schimmelreiter auf dem Aussendeich* (1941) on the cover of this book, and of the detail of a map by Johannes Mejer from Danckwerth's *Landesbeschreibung* (1652) which appears on page 10. To Dr David Jackson of the University of Wales College of Cardiff I owe special gratitude, for without his long and patient advice throughout the project its completion would not have been possible. I also thank Herr Fiete Pingel of the Nordfriisk Instituut, Bredstedt, for both his generous hospitality and his supply of useful historical material concerning the Hattstedt marsh region; the Westholsteinische Verlagsanstalt Boyens & Co., Heide, for permission to use a sketch-map by Professor Dr Karl Ernst Laage as a basis for the sketch-map of the setting of *Der Schimmelreiter* by Mrs Ruth Knight which appears on page 11; Dr Anja Kreutzer for her personal support and constant help with research; Herr Udo and Frau Helga Wiedersich, Herr Jürgen and Frau Fridegund Treede, Frau Anke Gehrhardt, Dr Rüdiger and Frau Heidi Sontag, Frau Marion Freund, Frau Corinna Schwartz and Frau Caren Brinckmann for their help during my visits to North Friesland and for their frequent kind provision of books, maps and photographic materials; Mrs Pamela Rayner, Mr David Stradling and Mr Stuart Nash for their critical reading of the final text. To my wife, Janet, my special thanks for her tireless support and encouragement during a long project and for walking the North Friesland dykes with me in the cold of winter. And to Frau Renate Capell and her family in whose house I first heard a reading of the story of the Deichgraf Hauke Haien, and where it all began.

Denis Jackson,
Cowes, March 1996

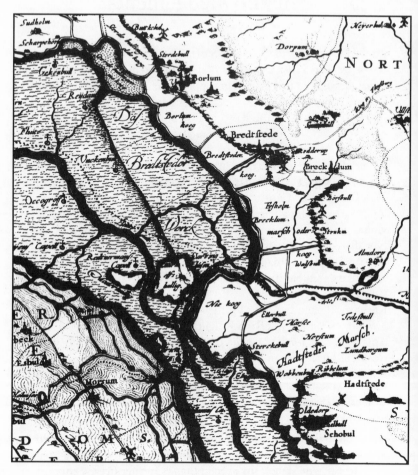

Detail of a map by the Husum cartographer Johannes
Mejer published in a survey of 1652, showing the west
coastline of the duchy of Schleswig before the flood of
1634. This is generally taken to be the map that Storm
used while writing *Der Schimmelreiter*; the topography
of the 'Nie koog' (lower centre), in particular, corre-
sponds closely to descriptions in the Novelle. (*Archiv der
Storm-Gesellschaft/Husum*)

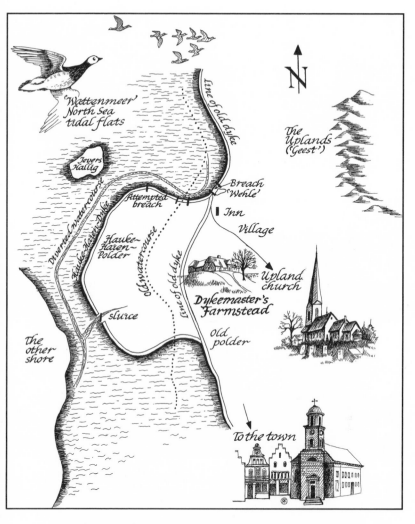

Redrawing of the area shown on Mejer's map of 1652 that is the presumed setting of *Der Schimmelreiter*. The 'upland church' is taken to be the St Marienkirche in Hattstedt, whose tower and spire were a familiar sight to Storm; the 'town' to be Husum, his birthplace, the 'other shore' that of the large island of Old Nordstrand, and 'Jevershallig' the former Harmelfshallig, 'lying a few thousand paces out across the shallows'. (*Ruth Knight*)

The Dykemaster

What I am about to relate is something I lighted upon a good fifty years ago at the house of my great-grandmother, old Frau Senator Feddersen, as I sat by her armchair reading a magazine bound in a thick blue cover; I can no longer remember whether it was the *Leipzig Journal* or *Pappe's Hamburg Digest*. I can still feel the caress of the over-eighty-year-old's gentle hand passing over her great-grandson's hair, and I still shudder with the horror of it. She and that era have long been buried; I have since tried to track down those pages, but in vain, and so I cannot guarantee the truth of the following account, nor could I vouch for the details should anyone wish to dispute them; I can only give my assurance that, although nothing has happened to call them back to mind, since that day I have never forgotten them.

It was in the third decade of the present century, on an October afternoon – so began the narrator of that time – when I rode along a North Friesian dyke in fierce weather. For more than an hour the desolate marsh, now cleared of all cattle, had been on my left, and on my right, uncomfortably close, the North Sea tidal flats. The Halligen and the other islands were normally to be seen from the dyke; but I now saw nothing but the yellow-grey waves beating continuously against the dyke as though bellowing with rage, from time to time spraying dirty spume over my horse and me, and further out, a bleak half-light in which it was impossible to tell earth from sky, for even the half-moon, now at its height, was more often than not hidden behind swirling dark clouds. It was icy cold; my frozen hands could hardly hold the reins, and I had every sympathy with the crows and gulls which, constantly cawing and cackling, were being driven inland by the storm. Dusk had begun to fall, and I could no longer make out my horse's hooves with certainty; I had not met a living soul, and heard nothing but the shrieking of birds as they almost brushed me and my trusty mare with their long wings, and the wild raging of the wind and the water. I do not deny that from time to time I longed for a safe haven.

The storm was now into its third day, and a particularly well-loved relative of mine had already kept me back too long on his farm in one of the northern parishes. Today I could delay no longer; I had business to attend to in town, which even now was still a good few hours to the south, and so, despite all the persuasive arts of my cousin and his kind wife, despite the farm's fine home-grown Perinette and Grand Richard apples waiting to be tasted, I had set off that afternoon. 'Just wait till you get to the sea,' my cousin had called after me from the door of his house, 'you'll be sure to turn back; we'll keep your room ready for you!'

And indeed, at the moment when a swathe of black cloud cast everything around me into pitch-darkness and howling squalls threatened to drive me and my mare off the dyke, the thought did cross my mind: 'Don't be a fool! Turn round and go back to the warmth and comfort of your relatives' home.' Then it occurred to me that the way back was probably further than the way forward to my destination; and so I trotted on, pulling my cloak collar up around my ears.

Something now came towards me along the dyke; I heard nothing; but when the half-moon cast its thin light I thought I made out a dark figure, and soon, as it came nearer, I saw it, it was riding a horse, a long-legged, lean grey; a dark cloak fluttered about the figure's shoulders, and as it sped past, a pair of burning eyes looked at me from a pallid face.

Who was he? What did he want? – It then occurred to me, I had heard no hoofbeats, no horse's panting; and horse and rider had passed close by!

Lost in thought I rode on, but I had little time for further reflection before it passed me again; this time from behind. I seemed to feel the streaming cloak brush against me and as on the first occasion the apparition flew by without a sound. Then I saw it further and further away from me; and then I thought I could see its shadow suddenly plunge down the landward side of the dyke.

With some hesitation I rode after it. When I had reached the spot, I saw in the polder below me, close by the side of the dyke, the gleaming water of a *Wehle* – the name they give here to craters that are gouged into the ground by the rush of water through a breach in a dyke and then mostly remain as small but very deep pools.

The surface of the water, even allowing for the protection of the dyke, was noticeably unruffled; the rider could not have disturbed it; I saw nothing more of him. But I did see something else, which I now heartily welcomed: in front of me, from across the polder below, came scattered gleams of shimmering light; they appeared to come from those low Friesian longhouses that stand isolated on high earthworks. Straight in front of me, half its height above the landward side of the dyke, stood a large house of this type; on its south side, to the right of the door, I saw all the windows lit; behind them I made out the forms of people and believed in spite of the storm that I could hear them. My horse of its own accord had already started down the track on the side of the dyke that led me to the door of the house. I saw without any doubt that it was an inn, for in front of the window I recognised the so-called *Ricks*, two posts supporting a beam with large iron rings for the tethering of livestock and horses that halted here.

I tethered my horse to one of these rings and handed it over to the ostler who approached me as I entered the hall. 'Is there a meeting going on here?' I inquired, as the clear sound of voices and clinking of glasses now came towards me from the guests' room.

'You could say that,' replied the ostler, speaking in Low German – which I learned later had been in use here alongside Friesian for over a hundred years – 'Dykemaster and members of the dyke committee, and some landowners from these parts. It's to do with the high tide!'

When I entered, I saw about a dozen men sitting round a table which ran full-length under the windows; a punchbowl stood on it, and a particularly imposing man appeared to be in charge.

I greeted them and asked if I might join them at the table, to which they readily agreed. 'You're keeping watch here then?' I said, turning to the man in charge. 'The weather's terrible outside; the dykes could be in danger!'

'Quite so,' he replied. 'But we believe we're out of danger here on the east side; it's only over there, on the other side, where it's not safe. Most of the dykes there are still of the old type; our main dyke here was rebuilt in the last century . . . We were beginning to feel the cold out there a short time ago,' he added, 'and it must have been the same for you. But we're going to have to weather it for a few more hours yet – we've got reliable men out there who keep us posted.' And before I could place my order with the landlord, a steaming glass had been placed in front of me.

I soon learned that my friendly neighbour was the dykemaster. We had fallen into conversation and I had begun telling him about my strange encounter on the dyke. He was most attentive, but suddenly I became aware that all talk around me had died away. 'The man on the grey!' cried one of the gathering, and a wave of alarm spread among the others.

The dykemaster stood up. 'There's no cause for alarm,' he said across the table. 'It's not just for us; in the year '17 it was for them on the other side too, and they'd better be prepared for it this time!'

A cold shiver had started down my spine. 'Excuse me!' I said, 'but what's this about the man on the grey?'

Away from the others behind the large stove sat a short, somewhat hunched, lean man in a black threadbare jacket; one of his shoulders appeared slightly misshapen. He had not contributed a word to the conversation, but his eyes, fringed with dark lashes which stood in stark contrast to the sparse grey hair on his head, clearly signalled that he was not here to doze.

The dykemaster stretched his hand towards him. 'Our schoolmaster,' he said in a raised voice, 'is the best one here to tell you the story; in his own way of course, and not as accurately as my old housekeeper Antje Vollmers would have told it at home.'

'I trust you are joking, dykemaster!' came the schoolmaster's somewhat frail voice from behind the stove, 'in comparing me with that stupid old crone of yours!'

'Of course, of course, schoolmaster!' the other replied, 'but perhaps old crones are the best at preserving stories of this kind!'

'No doubt!' said the little man; 'but it's clear we don't think alike on this matter,' and a superior smile spread across his keen features.

'You can see, can't you,' whispered the dykemaster in my ear, 'that he is still a touch arrogant; he studied theology in his youth, and it was only an unsuccessful courtship that got him stuck here in his home town as our schoolmaster.'

The man he spoke of had meanwhile moved away from his corner by the stove and seated himself next to me at the long table. 'Come on, schoolmaster, tell the story!' shouted a couple of the younger members of the group.

'Yes, of course,' he said, turning to me, 'I'll be glad to oblige; but there's a lot of superstition in this tale and leaving it out is quite an art .'

'I'll ask you not to leave it out,' I replied; 'just trust me to sift the wheat from the chaff!'

The old man cast me an appreciative smile. 'All right then!' he said, 'I'll begin. In the middle of the last century, or rather, to be more precise, both before and after that date, there was a dyke-master here who understood more about dykes and land drainage than any farmers or landowners normally cared to understand; yet even that would scarcely have been enough, for of all that the spe-cialists had written on such matters he had read little; what he knew he had thought out for himself from early childhood. You've no doubt heard, sir, that the Frieslanders are good at mathematics, and you will probably also have heard about our Hans Mommsen from Fahretoft, who was a farmer but could make mariners' com-passes and chronometers, telescopes and organs. Now, the father of this future dykemaster took after this man, if only in a small way. He had a few fens on which he cultivated rape and beans, he also grazed a cow, worked now and then as a land surveyor in the autumn and springtime, and in the winter, when the north-west gales came in from the sea and rattled his wooden shutters, sat in his room sketching and measuring. The boy mostly sat close by watching over the top of his school primer or Bible, running his fingers through his blond hair as his father measured and calcu-lated. One evening he asked the old man why it was that what he had just written down had to be that way and could not be set out differently, and offered his own suggestion. But his father, who had no answer, shook his head and said: "I can't tell you why it's

17

so; it just is, and you're wrong. But enough. If you really want to know more about it, go and look in the chest tomorrow, it's in the loft, look for that book, someone called Euclid wrote it – it'll tell you all you want to know!"

The following day the boy hurried up to the loft and soon found the book, for there were scarcely any books at all in the house; but his father laughed when he laid it on the table before him. It was a Dutch Euclid, and Dutch, although it was half-German, was not a language either of them understood. "Of course, of course," he said, "that's my father's book, he understood it; wasn't there a German one there?"

The boy, who was not given to saying much, looked calmly at his father and just said: "May I have it? There wasn't a German one."

And when the old man nodded the boy produced another book, a small one with some torn pages. "This one too?" he asked.

"Take them both!" said Tede Haien, "but they'll not be much use to you."

The second book was a small Dutch grammar, and since the winter had barely begun, when finally the gooseberries in their garden were again in flower he had read and understood almost all of the Euclid, which was a highly regarded text of that time.

I am aware, sir,' the narrator interrupted himself, 'that this same story is also told of our Hans Mommsen; but these stories were being told about Hauke Haien – as the boy was called – before Mommsen was born. And as you probably know, it only needs someone out of the ordinary to come along and everything, creditable or otherwise, that might have been done by his predecessors is attributed to him.

When the old man saw that the boy was not interested in cows or sheep, and barely noticed if the bean flowers were in bloom, which are a thing of great joy to every marshland farmer around here, and further considered that the smallholding could support a farmer and a young boy, but certainly not a semi-scholar and a farmhand, and that he himself had never actually prospered from it, he sent the growing lad out onto the dyke, where he had to work with others barrowing earth during the Easter to November season. "That'll cure him of his Euclid," he said quietly to himself.

And the youth went on barrowing earth; but he had the Euclid in his pocket all the time, and when the workers broke off work to have their breakfast or a break he sat on his upturned wheelbarrow with the book in his hand. When in the autumn the tides rose higher and often stopped the work, he did not go home with the others but would remain, hands folded across his knees, sitting on the sloping seaward side of the dyke, watching for hours as the turbulent waves of the North Sea beat higher and higher against the turf of the dyke; only when the water washed over his feet and the spume showered his face did he shuffle a few feet higher, then settle down again. He heard neither the splashing of the water nor the cries of the shore birds and seagulls which flew around or above him and nearly brushed him with their wings, their dark eyes flashing into his; neither did he see the night spread out over the broad, wild watery wasteland in front of him; he saw only how the foaming crests of the waves at high tide rained repeated heavy blows at the same spot and eroded the turfs on the steep dyke before his eyes.

After staring at the dyke for a long time he would very slowly nod his head, or without raising his eyes draw a smooth line in the air with his hand, as if he wanted to give a more gradual incline to the seaward slope of the dyke. And only when it became so dark that every earthly thing disappeared before his eyes and nothing but the sound of the waves thundered in his ears would he stand up and, almost soaked to the skin, trudge home.

When on one such evening he entered the room to see his father sitting cleaning his measuring instruments, the latter flew into a rage: "What were you doing out there? You could have drowned: the waters are biting into the dyke today."

Hauke looked at him defiantly.

"Didn't you hear what I said? I said you could have drowned."

"Yes," said Hauke, "but I didn't!"

"No," replied the old man after a while, looking straight at him as though lost in thought, "not this time."

"But," protested Hauke, "our dykes are useless!"

"What are you talking about?"

"The dykes, I said!"

"What about the dykes?"

"They're no good, father!" replied Hauke.

The old man laughed in his face. "What's all this then, my lad? Aren't you the wonder-boy from Lübeck!"

But the boy refused to be put off. "The seaward side is too steep," he said; "if the same thing happens again as it has more than once in the past, we could all be drowned here behind the dyke!"

The old man took his chewing tobacco from his pocket, twisted off a small plug and pushed it behind his teeth. "And how many barrow-loads have you moved today?" he asked angrily, for he saw clearly that even dyke work could not discourage the boy from study.

"Don't know, father," he said, "the same as the others; perhaps half a dozen more; but – the dykes must be changed!"

"Well," said the old man, starting to laugh, "perhaps you'll become dykemaster one day, then you can change them yourself!"

"Yes, father!" replied the boy.

The old man looked at him and swallowed a couple of times; then he went out of the room; he did not know how he should answer the boy.

* *

Although work on the dyke had finished at the end of October, the walk northwards towards the sea continued to be Hauke Haien's greatest pleasure; he looked forward to All Saints' Day as a child today would look forward to Christmas, to a time of year when the equinoctial storms usually rage, to a time – it is said – that is generally not welcomed in Friesland. Come a spring tide he was sure to be found, despite the wind and the weather, all alone far out on the dyke; and when the gulls cackled, when the waves raged against the dyke and rolled back ripping whole strips of turf off its grassy slope into the sea, then Hauke's angry laugh would be heard: "You're no good," he would shout into the noise of the wind; "just like human beings!" And finally, often in darkness, he would trudge home along the dyke away from the broad desolate wasteland until his lanky figure reached the low doorway under his father's reed-thatch roof and ducked beneath its arch to enter the small room.

Sometimes he brought home a handful of hard blue clay; then he would sit near the old man, who left him alone nowadays, and work it by the light of a thin tallow candle into all kinds of model dykes, which he then laid in a flat container filled with water, attempting to simulate the damaging action of the waves, or he would take his slate and draw how he thought the seaward side of the dyke should be shaped.

He never thought to associate with any of those who had sat beside him on the bench at school; neither, it appeared, had they much wish to be seen with a dreamer. When it was winter again, and the frost had set in, he walked even further out along the dyke, further than he had ever been before, until the vast ice-covered expanse of the tidal flats lay before him.

In February during persistent frosty weather, corpses were discovered washed up on the shore; they had lain out in the sound on the frozen mudflats. A young woman who had been there when the bodies were brought into the village stood talking excitedly in front of old Tede Haien. "Don't imagine they looked like humans," she cried; "no, more like sea-devils! Such huge heads, I tell you!" and she held her splayed hands and fingers wider apart, "as black as pitch and glistening, like newly-baked bread! And the shrimps had nibbled at them – the children screamed when they saw them."

Such things were not exactly new to old Tede Haien. "Most likely they've been drifting in the sea since November," he said calmly.

Hauke stood quietly next to them, but as soon as he could he stole away to the dyke; it was hard to say whether he wanted to look for other corpses or was simply drawn by the horror that still pervaded the now deserted places where the bodies had lain. He walked further and further until he stood alone amid the desolate wasteland where only the winds blew over the dyke, where there was nothing but the plaintive calls of the large birds that flew swiftly overhead; on his left was the vast empty marshland, and on his right the shimmering, ice-covered surface of the vast tidal flats; it was as though the whole world lay in a white death.

Hauke stood still on the dyke and his sharp eyes scanned the

21

shore before him; but there were no signs of further bodies; only where the hidden currents flowed beneath the flats did the surface of the ice rise and fall in stream-like patterns from the pressures beneath.

He walked home, but on one of the very next evenings he was out again on the dyke. In those same places the ice was now cracked, and it rose up like billowing smoke from out of the fissures, a blanket of vapour and fog spreading itself out over the entire surface of the flats and blending strangely with the evening twilight. Hauke stared long and hard at it; for within the mist dark forms were striding back and forth and they appeared to be as tall as people. He saw them far in the distance walking to and fro along the steaming fissures; dignified, yet with strange frightening gestures and with long noses and necks. Suddenly they began to jump about weirdly like clowns, the tallest over the shortest and the smallest against the biggest; then they grew larger and lost all form.

"What are they up to? Are they the ghosts of drowned men?" Hauke wondered. "Ahoy!" he cried out into the night; but those who were out there ignored his call and carried on with their strange antics.

There came into his mind the terrifying Norwegian sea spirits an old sea captain had once told him about which, instead of faces, had short thick mops of seagrass projecting from the nape of their necks. But he did not run away; instead he dug the heels of his boots firmly into the clay on the dyke and looked straight at the grotesque shapes which disported themselves in front of his eyes in the gathering twilight. "So you're here too, are you?" he said in a firm voice. "You're not going to frighten me away!"

Only when everything was shrouded in darkness did he slowly turn his steps towards home. Closely following him came sounds like the swishing of wings and echoing cries. He did not look round, but neither did he quicken his pace, and it was quite late when he arrived home; it is said that he never told his father, nor anyone else, about what he had seen. It was not until many years later, at the same time of day and year, that he took up onto the dyke with him the mentally retarded child with whom the Lord was later to burden him, and those same creatures were said to have appeared again out on the mudflats; but he told her not to be afraid because they were only grey herons and crows that appeared so big and terrible in the fog; they were pulling fish out of the open fissures in the ice.

God knows, sir!' said the schoolmaster, interrupting his tale, 'there are all kinds of things on this earth that can confound an honest Christian soul, but Hauke was neither a fool nor an idiot.'

As I did not reply, he was about to continue when a sudden commotion arose among the other guests who until now had been listening without a sound amid the thickening haze of tobacco smoke that filled the low-ceilinged room; first the odd one or two, then nearly all of them moved towards the window. Outside – they could be seen through the uncurtained windows – the clouds were being driven by the storm, and light and darkness chased each other across the sky in confusion; even I was sure I had seen the gaunt rider rushing by on his grey.

'Wait a moment, schoolmaster!' said the dykemaster in a low voice.

'There's no need to be afraid, dykemaster!' said the little narrator, 'I've said nothing to offend him, nor have I cause to,' and he looked up at the dykemaster with his small, intelligent eyes.

'No, no of course not,' said the other, 'but let's get that glass of yours filled up again.' And after this was done and the other listeners had returned, most of them with somewhat disconcerted expressions, he continued with his story:

'So, preferring only the company of the wind and the water and scenes of solitude about him, Hauke grew up into a tall lean youth. He had been confirmed for well over a year when the course of his life suddenly changed; and it came about through the old white Angora tomcat that old Trin' Jans' ill-fated son had once brought back with him from his voyage to Spain. Trin' lived in a small thatched cottage a good way out on the dyke, and whenever the old woman busied herself about the house this monster of a tomcat would sit in front of the cottage door and blink at the summer days and the lapwings as they flew over. When Hauke passed by, the tom would miaul at him and he would nod in response; the two could read each other's thoughts.

One spring day Hauke was following his habit of lying on the seaward slope of the dyke some way down towards the water's edge among the pink thrift and the fragrant sea-wormwood and letting himself be warmed by the already strong sun. The day before he had collected pocketfuls of pebbles from the uplands above the marsh, and when the low tide exposed the mudflats and the little grey sandpipers called and scurried across them, he suddenly pulled a stone from his pocket and threw it at the birds. He had practised this from an early age and usually one of them remained lying out on the mud; but he was not always able to walk out and fetch it, and Hauke had thought of taking the tom-cat with him to train as a retriever, but there were the occasional firm stretches of mud or sand where he was well able to walk out over the flats and retrieve the quarry himself. Should the tom still be sitting by the front door on his return, it would yowl from unconcealed greed until Hauke threw it a bird from the bag.

When today, with his jacket slung over his shoulder, he carried home a bird which he could not readily identify although its feathers were colourful with a silky metallic hue, the large tom miauled as usual when it saw him coming. But this time Hauke wanted to keep his catch to himself – it might well have been a kingfisher – so he ignored the animal's greed. "Turn and turn about!" he shouted. "Mine today, yours tomorrow. This isn't cat food, my friend!" But the cat crept stealthily up to him; Hauke stood and looked at it, the bird dangling from his hand, and the cat stopped with a paw raised in the air. The young lad, however, evidently did not know his feline friend so well, for just as he turned his back on it to go on his way, he felt a sudden jolt as the spoil was snatched from his hand, and at the same time a sharp claw tore into his flesh. A rage like a wild beast's coursed through his veins, and turning swiftly he grabbed the thief violently by the scruff of its neck. Holding the mighty animal up in the air, he choked it with his fist so that its eyes bulged out of its coarse hair – totally unaware that its strong hind-claws were ripping into the flesh of his arm. "Oho!" he shouted, gripping it even tighter, "we'll soon see which one of us can keep this up the longest!"

The large cat's hind legs suddenly went limp; Hauke stepped back a few paces, then hurled the cat against the wall of the old woman's cottage. When it did not move, he turned and resumed his walk homewards.

The Angora tomcat, however, was its mistress's pride and joy; it was her sole companion and the only thing that her son, a seaman, had left her after meeting with sudden death on this coast setting out to help his mother with her shrimp fishing during a storm. Hauke had hardly gone a hundred paces, dabbing the blood from his wounds with a handkerchief, when howling and wailing from the cottage met his ears. He turned and saw the old woman lying on the ground in front of the cottage; her grey hair flew in the wind about her red headscarf. "Dead!" she cried, "dead!" and raised her thin arm threateningly towards him: "Curse you, Hauke Haien! You've beaten him to death, you good-for-nothing beachcomber! You weren't even fit to stroke his tail!" She threw herself over the animal and with her apron gently wiped away the blood that ran from its nose and mouth, then renewed her wailing.

"Are you going to stop soon?" he shouted at her. "Let me tell you something: I'll get you another tom, but he will have to be satisfied with mice and rats' blood!"

Seemingly unshaken, he went on his way. But the thought of the dead cat must have confused him, for when he arrived at the houses not only did he walk past his own father's, but also passed the others, and continued to walk further south along the dyke towards the town.

Trin' Jans, meanwhile, was also walking along the top of the dyke in the same direction; she was cradling something in an old blue-checked pillowcase as if it were a small child; her grey hair blew gently in the light spring wind. "What are you lugging there, Trin'?" asked a farmer coming towards her. "More than your house and farm are worth together," replied the old woman, and went determinedly on her way. When she came nearer to Hauke's father's house, which lay below the dyke, she turned off down an *Akt* – the name we give in these parts to a path or animal track that leads down the side of a dyke to the houses below.

Old Tede Haien was at that moment standing by the door looking at the weather. "Well, Trin'!" he said, when she stood breathlessly before him, pressing her crooked stick into the ground. "Something interesting in that sack of yours?"

"First let me into your room, Tede Haien! Then you shall see right enough!", and there was a strange gleam in her eyes.

25

"Come in then!" said the old man. What did he care about the look in the stupid old woman's eyes?

When they were both inside, she continued: "Take that old tobacco tin and those writing things off the table . . . What've you got so much to write about, anyway? . . . There, and now wipe the top clean!"

And the old man, who was growing curious, did everything she said; then she took the blue pillowcase by two of its corners and shook the large tomcat's dead body out onto the table. "There! Now you can see!" she shouted. "Your Hauke's beaten him to death." Then she began to cry bitterly; she stroked the dead animal's thick coat, placed its paws together, and leaned her long nose over its head, whispering indistinct endearments into its ears.

"So," said Tede Haien, looking on, "Hauke's beaten him to death, has he?" He was not sure how he should deal with the hysterical old woman.

The old woman nodded angrily. "As God's my witness, that's what he did all right!" she said, wiping the moisture from her eyes with her deformed arthritic hand. "No child anymore; not a living soul!" she lamented. "And you know how it is with us old folk after All Saints' Day when our legs freeze in bed at night, and instead of sleeping we listen to the north-west wind rattling our old shutters. I don't like hearing that, Tede Haien; it blows from where my boy sank in the mud."

Tede Haien nodded and the old woman stroked the dead cat's coat. "During the winters," she continued, "when I sat at my spinning wheel, he would come and sit by me, purr, and look at me with his green eyes! And when it was cold and I crawled into bed – he wouldn't take long, he would jump up after me and lie there on my freezing cold legs and we would sleep so warmly together; it was as if my dear boy were still in bed with me!" The old woman, as though seeking sympathy with these reminiscences, looked at the old man with her eyes flashing as he stood next to her at the table.

Tede Haien thought for a while. "Let me put this to you, Trin' Jans," he said, and he went to his coffer and took a silver coin from its drawer. "You say Hauke beat your cat to death and I know you're not a liar. Well, here's a Christian the Fourth crown

26

piece, use it to buy yourself a tanned lambskin for those cold old legs of yours! And when our cat has her next litter you can select the biggest for yourself, that will more than make up for a mangy old Angora tomcat! Now for goodness' sake take this animal and give it to the knacker in the town and don't tell a soul it's lain here on my respectable table!"

While the old man was still speaking, the woman had grabbed the coin and put it safely away in a small purse that she carried beneath her skirts; then she stuffed the tomcat back into the pillowcase, wiped away the spots of blood off the table with her apron, and stalked out of the room. "Mind you don't forget about the young tom!" she called back.

A while later, as old Tede Haien was pacing up and down in the narrow room, Hauke came in and threw the richly coloured bird onto the table; but when he saw the still discernible bloodstains on its cleanly-scrubbed surface, he asked, almost casually: "What's this then?"

His father stood still: "That blood is your doing!"

The youth's face suddenly reddened. "Has Trin' Jans been here with her tomcat?"

The old man nodded: "Why did you have to beat it to death?"

Hauke revealed his blood-stained arm. "That's why!" he retorted; "it snatched the bird away from me!"

The old man did not respond but continued to pace up and down for a while. Lost in thought, he stopped in front of the boy, gazed at him for a moment, then said: "I've settled the matter of the cat – but look, Hauke, this cottage, it's really too small for both of us; two men's too many – it's about time you found yourself a job with someone!"

"I know, father," replied Hauke; "I've been thinking the same thing myself."

"Why's that?" asked the old man.

"Because some real work's needed to get rid of the anger that boils up inside."

"Ah!" said the old man, "so that's why you beat the cat to death, is it? It could easily have led to worse things – you know that!"

"You might be right, father . . . By the way, the dykemaster's dismissed his farmhand: there's a job I could do!"

The old man resumed his pacing up and down, spitting out black tobacco juice onto the floor. "The dykemaster's an idiot, as stupid as they come. He's only dykemaster because his father and grandfather were dykemasters before him and because of the twenty-nine fens he owns. When Martinmas comes round and the dyke and sluice accounts have to be finished, he dines the schoolmaster on roast goose, mead and wheat crackers and sits beside him and nods when he runs his quill down the rows of figures, and says: 'That's it, that's it, schoolmaster. God bless you! You are good at figures, aren't you?' If, though, the schoolmaster can't do it, or won't for some reason, and he's got to do it himself, then he sits and scribbles, then rubs it out again, and the great oaf goes all hot and red, and his eyes bulge like large marbles as though his tiny bit of intelligence is about to burst out of his skull."

The young man rose to his feet in front of his father, startled at such a torrent of words; he had never heard him speak in that way before. "Yes, God knows, he's stupid all right," he said; "but his daughter Elke – she's good at figures!"

The old man gave him a sharp look. "Heh, Hauke," he exclaimed, "what do you know about Elke Volkerts?"

"Nothing, father; the schoolmaster told me about her, that's all."

The old man did not respond; he simply shifted the plug of tobacco he was chewing, carefully, from behind one cheek to behind the other.

"And you believe," he said, "that you'd also be able to help out with the figures over there?'

"I'm sure of it, father," said his son, and a serious expression played around his lips.

The old man shook his head: "Well then, I think you should go and try your luck!'

'Thank you, father!' said Hauke, and climbed up to his sleeping quarters in the loft, sat down on the edge of the bed, and mused on his father's abrupt reaction to his mention of Elke Volkerts. He knew her, certainly, that slim eighteen-year-old with the narrow, dark-complexioned face and dark eyebrows closely knit above defiant eyes and a slender nose, but as yet he had hardly ever spoken a word to her; now if he were to go to old Tede Volkerts, he would take a much closer look at her to see what kind of girl she really was. And he wanted to go at once so that no one else could snatch the job away from him; it was still hardly evening. He put on his Sunday jacket and best boots and strode off in good spirits.

The dykemaster's Friesian longhouse could already be seen from afar, for it stood on a high earthwork beside the tallest tree in the village, a mighty ash. The present dykemaster's grandfather, the first dykemaster in the family, had planted a similar tree in his youth on the east side of the door, but the first two plantings came to nothing so, on the morning of his wedding, he planted this third tree which today, with its ever-spreading crown of leaves, rustled here in the incessant wind just as in times gone by.

After a while, the tall lean figure of Hauke was climbing the high earthwork whose sides were planted with beet and cabbage; he saw up ahead of him the dykemaster's daughter standing beside the low door of the house. One of her slender arms hung loosely at her side while her other hand gripped one of the two iron rings that were behind her on the wall, one on each side of the door, so that whoever rode up to the house could tether his horse. From where he was standing the girl appeared to be look- ing out over the dyke towards the sea where, on this calm evening, the sun had begun to set below the water and was bathing the dark-complexioned girl in gold with its last rays.

Hauke slowed his pace as he climbed the earthwork and thought to himself: "She doesn't look at all stupid!" Then he reached the top. "Evening, Fräulein Elke!" he said, walking up towards her; "what's that you're looking at?"

"Oh, something that happens here every evening," she replied, "but you can't often see it as clearly as this." She released the iron ring from her hand so that it clanged against the wall behind her. "What brings you up here then, Hauke Haien?" she asked.

"Something you won't mind, I hope," he said. "I heard that your father's got rid of his farmhand, so I thought I might just try for the job myself."

She looked him up and down. "You're still a bit skinny though, Hauke!" she said; "although a pair of sharp eyes will be of more use to us around here than a pair of strong arms, I can tell you!" All the while she was looking almost forbiddingly at him, but Hauke would not be put off. "Come on then," she continued, "the master's in the living room, let's go in!"

✳ ✳

Next day Tede Haien and his son stepped into the dykemaster's spacious living room. The visitor's eye was delighted by walls decorated with glazed tiles; some showed a ship under full sail, others an angler by the shore or a cow ruminating before a farmhouse. This permanent wall-covering was interrupted by an imposing recessed box-bed, its doors now closed, and a wall cupboard through the glass doors of which all kinds of china and silverware could be seen. Beside the door to the adjoining guests' room, set into the wall behind a pane of glass, was a Dutch striking clock.

The stout, somewhat apoplectic-looking master of the house was seated on a brightly coloured woollen cushion in an armchair at the head of a cleanly scrubbed table. His hands were folded over his paunch and his round eyes were staring contentedly at the carcase of a fat duck; knife and fork rested on the plate before him.

"Good morning, dykemaster!" said Haien, and the man addressed slowly turned his head towards him.

"Is that you, Tede?" he replied, in a voice replete with consumption of the fat duck. "Come and sit down. It's a good stretch from your place to mine!"

"I've come, dykemaster," said Tede Haien, seating himself opposite the other on a bench that ran along the wall, "because I hear you've had some trouble with your farmhand and have come to an agreement with my son for him to take his place."

The dykemaster nodded: "Yes I have, Tede, but – what do you mean by 'trouble'? We marsh folk, God preserve us, can deal with that sort of thing!" and he took the knife lying before him and affectionately tapped the carcase of the poor duck. "That was my favourite bird," he added with a contented smile; "it used to eat out of my hand!"

"I thought," said old Haien, ignoring the last remark, "the rascal had been causing havoc in your stable."

"Havoc? Yes, Tede; certainly havoc enough! The fool didn't

provide the calves with milk; instead lay dead drunk in the hayloft, and the animals bellowed the whole night from thirst, I needed to sleep in until midday to make up for it; a farm can't be run like that!"

"Of course not, dykemaster; but there's no risk of that with my son."

Hauke stood by the door with hands in his pockets, head raised, studying the window frames opposite.

The dykemaster looked across at him and nodded. "Of course not, Tede," he said, turning towards the old man, "your Hauke will not disturb my night's rest; the schoolmaster told me some time ago that he prefers to sit with an abacus in front of him rather than a glass of brandy."

Hauke heard nothing of this compliment, for Elke had walked into the room and was quietly gathering up the remains of the meal from the table with her light deft hand, casting him fleeting glances with her dark eyes. It was then he noticed her. "My God," he said to himself, "she's a good-looking one!"

The girl left the room. "You know, Tede," continued the dykemaster, "the Lord has denied me a son!"

"I know, dykemaster, but don't let that grieve you," replied the other, "for it's said that hereditary intelligence dries up by the third generation; your grandfather, as we all rightly know, was one of those who protected the land!"

The dykemaster, after a moment's thought, looked taken aback. "What do you mean by that, Tede Haien?" he said, sitting up in his armchair: "I am the third generation!"

"Indeed so! But don't take it amiss, dykemaster; it's just one of those sayings!" And the lean figure of Tede Haien looked at the old office-bearer with a somewhat malicious glint in his eyes.

The dykemaster went on unperturbed: "You shouldn't believe such old wives' tales, Tede Haien; you just don't know my daughter, that's all. She can run rings round me when it comes to figures, I can tell you! I will only say that your Hauke, besides working in the fields, will also learn a good deal here in my room with that quill or slate-pencil of his that certainly won't do him any harm!"

"Of course, dykemaster, he'll certainly do that, you're quite right," said old Haien, and then began to stipulate a few conces-

sions that should form part of the employment contract, conces-
sions that had not been thought of by his son the evening before.
As a supplement to his wages the boy was to receive, besides his
linen shirts in the autumn, eight pairs of woollen stockings; old
Haien also wanted to have Hauke for a week in the spring to do
his own work; and so on. The dykemaster agreed to all these con-
cessions; Hauke Haien appeared to him to be the ideal farmhand.

"Heaven help you, my lad," said old Haien, as soon as they
had left the house, "if he's the one to show you your way in the
world!"

But Hauke replied calmly: "Don't worry, father; it's going to
be all right."

✶ ✶

And Hauke was not far wrong; the world, or what it meant to
him, became clearer the longer he stayed in the house; perhaps all
the clearer the less a superior intellect was there to help him, and
the more he had to rely on his own resources which had supported him all along. There was, however, someone in the household
who was not well disposed towards Hauke: that was the head-
farmhand Ole Peters, a good worker and a fellow with a clever
tongue. The previous indolent and stupid but sturdy farmhand
had been more to his liking; he had easily been able to load a full
barrel of oats on his back and bully him to his heart's content.
But he could not do the same to the quieter Hauke, who was
intellectually superior to him; Hauke had a particular way of
looking at him. Nevertheless, Ole Peters knew how to select jobs
for him that could have been harmful to his incompletely developed body, and when the head-farmhand remarked: "You should
have seen that fat Niss set about it, it was easy for him!" Hauke
would summon every ounce of his strength and finish the job,
however difficult he found it. It was fortunate for him that Elke
herself, or through her father, managed to put a stop to this most
of the time. One might ask what it is that unites total strangers
from time to time; perhaps they were both born mathematicians
and the girl could not stand seeing her companion harmed by
such heavy labour.

The conflict between the head-farmhand and Hauke did not

32

disappear in the winter when the various dyke accounts came in for auditing after St Martin's Day.

It was a May evening with November weather; from inside the house the thunder of the breakers could be heard behind the dyke outside. "Heh, Hauke!" said the master of the house, "come in; now you can show us whether you're good at figures!"

"But Squire," replied Hauke – for that is what people call their employer in these parts – "I've got to feed the young cattle first."

"Elke!" called the dykemaster; "where are you, Elke! – Go and tell Ole he's to feed the young cattle: Hauke's to work on some figures!"

Elke hurried to the stable and conveyed the message to the head-farmhand who was busy at that moment hanging up the harnesses that had been used during the day.

Ole Peters struck out with a snaffle rein at one of the railings close to where he was working as though he wanted to smash it to pieces: "To hell with that damned scribbler!"

She caught the words before she had closed the stable door.

"Well?" asked the old man, as she entered the room.

"Ole wanted to take care of it himself," said his daughter, biting her lip a little and sitting down opposite Hauke on a roughly carved wooden chair, such as people still made for themselves at home at that time during the long winter evenings. She had taken a white stocking with a red bird pattern on it out of a drawer, which she now continued to knit; the long-legged creatures on it might well have been meant to represent herons or storks. Hauke sat opposite, engrossed in his calculations; the dykemaster rested in his armchair, blinking sleepily across at Hauke's quill; on the table, as always in the dykemaster's house, burned two tallow candles, and the shutters to both leaded windows were bolted on the outside and fastened together on the inside; the wind could now blow as much as it liked. Occasionally Hauke lifted his head from his work and glanced across for a moment at the bird-patterned stocking or at the girl's fine, composed face.

From the direction of the armchair came a sudden loud snore, and a glance and a smile flitted between the two young people; then gradually a quieter breathing followed, and there was a chance to chat a little, only Hauke did not know what to say.

But when she lifted up her knitting and the birds were revealed at full length, he whispered to her across the table: "Where did you learn to do that, Elke?"

"Learn to do what?" she answered in return.

"Knit bird patterns," he said.

"Oh, that? From Trin' Jans out on the dyke, she can do all sorts of things. A long time ago she was once here in service with my grandfather."

"You weren't even born then?" said Hauke.

"I should think not; but she's often been to this house since."

"Does she like birds then?" Hauke asked; "I thought she was keen on cats!"

Elke shook her head: "She breeds and sells ducks. But last spring when you beat her Angora to death the rats did a lot of damage to them at the back of her pen, and now she wants to build another one for herself at the front of the house."

"Ah," said Hauke, and whistled quietly through his teeth, "that's why she dragged clay and stones here all the way from the uplands! But she'll be on the inner path! – Has she got permission?"

"Don't know," said Elke. But Hauke had spoken the last word so loudly that the dykemaster was startled from his slumber.

"What permission?" he asked, looking almost wildly from one to the other. "Permission for what?"

But when Hauke had explained the situation to him, he laughed and patted him on the shoulder: "What of it, the inner path of the dyke is wide enough: Heaven help dykemasters, do they have to worry themselves about duck pens as well!"

Hauke felt such a twinge of conscience for having left the old woman with her young ducks to the mercy of the rats that he let the matter rest. "But Squire," he began again, "a bit of telling-off might do one or two people some good, and if you won't do it yourself you should get onto the member of the dyke committee who is responsible for the state of the dyke!"

"What, what's the lad saying?" and the dykemaster sat up with a jerk. Elke lowered her finely worked stocking to listen to what Hauke was saying.

"Well, Squire," continued Hauke, "you've already finished the spring inspection of the dykes but Peter Jansen still hasn't cleared the weeds from his patch; once again the goldfinches will have

34

their fun and games there in the summer among the purple thistle heads! And very close by – I don't know who it belongs to – there's a large hollow on the seaward side of the dyke, it's always full of small children in good weather, they play around in it; but God protect us from a high tide!"

The eyes of the old dykemaster had grown larger and larger.

"And then –" continued Hauke.

"And then what, my lad?" asked the dykemaster; "haven't you finished yet?" and it sounded as though his farmhand's talk had already become too much for him.

"And then, Squire," Hauke went on; "you know that fat Vollina, the daughter of Harders on the dyke committee, who always fetches her father's horses in from the fen – well, when she's on the old light-brown mare with her bulging calves and tells it to 'giddyup!' she rides it every time diagonally up the side of the dyke!"

Only now did Hauke notice that Elke had directed her intelligent eyes towards him and was slowly shaking her head.

He fell silent, but the crash of the old man's fist on the table suddenly rang in his ears: "The weather will drive its way into the dyke there!" he shouted, and Hauke was shocked by the sudden growl in his voice. "Fine her! Note that down for me, Hauke; the fat hussy's got to be fined! She's the slut who stole three young ducks from me last summer! Yes, yes, make a note of it," he repeated as Hauke hesitated. "I even believe it was four!"

"Oh father," said Elke; "wasn't it the otter that took the ducks?"

"Some otter!" exclaimed the old man with a snort. "I can tell the difference between that fat Vollina and an otter! No, no, four ducks, Hauke, four ducks – but to return to what you were chattering about, in the spring the chief dykemaster and I, after we had had breakfast together here in this house, we went past those weeds and that hollow of yours and we couldn't see a thing. But you two," and he nodded purposefully a few times at Hauke and his daughter, "should thank God you're not dykemaster! A man's only got one pair of eyes, but he's expected to have a hundred. – Take a close look at the dyke repair accounts, Hauke, the straw laying and fixing. Those fellows' figures are often imaginative!"

He sank back again into his armchair, shifted his heavy body a few times, and had soon surrendered himself to untroubled slumber.

* *

The same scene was repeated on many a subsequent evening. Hauke had sharp eyes and whenever the three of them sat together he never missed the opportunity to draw the old man's attention to this or that case of damage or omission involving the dykes; and since the old man could not always close his eyes to these, a more active administrative style unexpectedly came to the management of the dykes, and those who under the former easy-going system had persistently offended against the rules and now suddenly found their knuckles being rapped for dishonesty or idleness, began to look around, indignant and astonished, to see from which quarter the blows had come. And Ole Peters, the head-farmhand, did not delay in spreading what he knew about Hauke as widely as possible, stirring up resentment against Hauke and his father who, after all, had to bear his share of the blame; others, however, who were not directly affected or who were concerned primarily with the issue itself, simply laughed and derived some pleasure from the youth's having stirred the old man to action for once. "It's a shame," they said, "that the young rascal doesn't have enough clay under his feet, for then we might have had a dykemaster one day like the ones we had in the past; but those few acres of his father's are nowhere near enough!"

When in the following autumn the district's Amtmann and chief dykemaster was on his tour of inspection, he looked old Tede Volkerts up and down over breakfast and said: "I'm quite certain, dykemaster, that you've become at least ten years younger. The proposals you are making have quite worn me out for the moment – if only we could get through them all today!"

"Of course we can, of course we can, Your Honour," replied the old man, smiling benignly; "the roast goose there will certainly do the trick! Yes, thank God, I'm still hale and hearty as ever!" He looked around the room to be sure that Hauke was not within hearing range, then added with pompous gravity: "And I trust to God that I shall be able to carry out my duties for a few more years yet."

"To that, my dear dykemaster," replied his superior, standing up, "we'll drink a toast!"

And as the glasses were clinking, Elke, who had been serving them breakfast, went out through the living room door laughing quietly to herself. She took a bowl of scraps from the kitchen and went through to the stable to throw them to the poultry outside the main doors. Hauke was standing in the stable forking hay into the hayracks for the cows which had just been brought in because of the appalling weather. When he saw the girl coming towards him, however, he stuck his fork into the ground. "Hello, Elke!" he said.

The girl stopped and nodded to him: "Oh, Hauke; you really should have been here just now!"

"What do you mean, Elke? What for?"

"The chief dykemaster praised my father!"

"Your father? What's that to do with me?"

"No, what I meant was – he praised the dykemaster!"

The young man's face went bright red: "I think I know what you're driving at," he said.

"There's no need to blush, Hauke. You're the one the chief dykemaster really praised."

Hauke looked at her with a half-smile. "You as well, Elke!" he said.

But she shook her head: 'No, Hauke. When I used to help out alone here, there was never any praise; I can simply do the accounts, that's all. But you see everything that's going on around you – things that the dykemaster should be seeing for himself; you've pushed me to one side!"

"I never wanted to do that, least of all to you," said Hauke shyly, shoving the head of a cow to one side. "Come on, Scarlet, don't eat the fork; you want everything!"

"Don't think I regret it, Hauke," said the girl after a moment's thought. "It's a man's job really!"

Hauke stretched an arm towards her: "Give me your hand on that, Elke!"

The girl went a deep red beneath her dark eyebrows. "What for? I'm not lying!" she cried.

Hauke prepared to answer; but she had already left the stable, and he stood with the fork in his hand and heard only the noise of the ducks and the hens outside as they gabbled and clucked around her.

✻ ✻

It was January in Hauke's third year of service, and a winter contest known here as "Eisboseln" was to be held. A persistent frost during a lull in the coastal winds had covered all the ditches between the fens with a firm, smooth surface of crystal so that the divided plots of land now became one wide lane suitable for the throwing of small lead-filled wooden balls until a distant target had been struck. Day in, day out, a light wind blew from the north-east: everything had been arranged; the upland folk from a parish to the east beyond the marsh, who had won last year, had been challenged to a contest and had accepted; each side had put forward nine throwers; even the umpire of the contest and the team spokesmen had been nominated. The latter, who had to negotiate with each other in cases of argument over a doubtful throw, were usually selected from those best able to present their case in the most favourable light, preferably young fellows, who had the gift of the gab in addition to common sense. Foremost among these was Ole Peters, the dykemaster's head-farmhand. "Just throw like hell," he said; "and leave the talking to me!"

It was towards evening on the day before the contest; in an ante-room of the upland village inn, a number of the throwers had gathered to consider the admission of some last-minute applicants for the teams. Hauke Haien was among these; he had not wanted to be at first although he was confident of his skill at throwing; but he was afraid of being rejected by Ole Peters who held an honorary position in the contest, and he wanted to spare himself the shame of it. Elke had changed his mind at the eleventh hour: "He won't dare do it, Hauke," she had said; "he's a day-labourer's son; your father's got livestock as well as being the cleverest man in the village!"

"But what if he does?"

She looked at him with a flicker of a smile in her dark eyes. "Then," she said, "he'll have a shock coming to him if he thinks he's going to dance with his boss's daughter in the evening!" – and Hauke had bravely nodded his agreement to her.

The young lads who still wanted to be in the contest now stood freezing and stamping their feet outside the village inn, looking up at the spire on the broad, stone church tower that

38

stood nearby. The pastor's doves, which fed off the fields around the village in the summer, were coming in from the yards and barns of neighbouring farms where they had been searching for their corn, and were disappearing under the shingles of the tower behind which they had their nests; a glowing sunset lay over the sea to the west.

"It'll be fine tomorrow!" said one of the young lads, and began to stamp up and down to keep warm; "but cold! cold!" Another, when he did not see any more doves flying around, went into the inn and stood listening by the door to the ante-room from which the animated sound of disputing voices reverberated; the dyke-master's farmhand had also gone in to join him. "Listen, Hauke," said the lad to him, "they're arguing about you now!" and Ole Peter's rasping voice could clearly be heard: "Farmhands and young lads don't belong in this contest!"

"Come," whispered the lad and sought to pull Hauke by the sleeve of his jacket closer to the door. "You can learn how much they think of you from here!"

But Hauke tore himself loose and went to stand outside the inn again. "They haven't shut us out so that we can stand and listen to what's going on!" he shouted back.

In front of the inn stood the third applicant. "I'm afraid there's a hitch in my case," he called to Hauke. "I'm under eighteen; let's hope they don't want to see my baptism certificate! But Hauke, your head-farmhand will be sure to talk them round for you!"

"Yes, and out of it!" growled Hauke and kicked a stone across the street with his foot. "Certainly not into it!"

The din in the room grew louder, then gradually died away; those outside once more heard the light north-east wind sweeping against the spire above. The eavesdropper returned to the others. "Who've they chosen then?" asked the eighteen-year-old.

"Him there!" said the boy, pointing at Hauke. "Ole Peters wanted to count him among the youngsters; but they all shouted him down. 'His father's got cattle and land,' said Jess Hansen. 'Yes, land,' shouted Ole Peters, 'which thirteen barrows could easily cart away!' Finally Ole Hensen spoke. 'Quiet, all of you!' he shouted; 'I'll teach you something: tell me, who's the top man in the village?' At first they didn't say anything, they seemed to be thinking about it. Then a voice said: 'Of course, must be the dykemaster!' And all the others began to shout: 'Yes, no doubt about it, the dykemaster!' – 'And who's the real dykemaster around here?' repeated Ole Hensen, 'and this time think carefully about it!' At that moment someone began to chuckle quietly, and then another, until finally the whole room was in an uproar. 'In which case,' said Ole Hensen, 'let's have him, don't turn the dykemaster away from the door!' I think they're still laughing in there; but you can't hear Ole Peter's voice any more!" So the boy ended his report.

Almost at the same time the ante-room door in the inn was thrown open, and: "Hauke! Hauke Haien!" rang out loud and jubilant into the cold night air.

Then Hauke went into the inn and heard nothing more about who the real dykemaster was; what was then on his mind no one has ever managed to discover.

Some while later as he approached his employer's house he saw Elke standing further down the earthwork near the wooden gate that led to the fens; the moonlight shimmered over the immeasurable expanse of white frozen pasture. "Still here, Elke?" he asked.

She simply nodded. "Well, what happened then?" she asked. "Did he dare try it?"

"He certainly did!"

"And?"

"Everything's fine, Elke; I can throw tomorrow!"

"Good night, Hauke!" And she ran swiftly up the earthwork and disappeared into the house.

Hauke slowly followed her.

✳ ✳

On the following afternoon, on the wide expanse of pasture land that stretched to the east along the landward side of the dyke, a dark throng of people was to be seen standing motionless; then, after two loaded wooden balls had flown out of it over ground from which the day's sun had lifted the hoarfrost, it moved gradually further away from the low longhouses behind it. The teams' throwers in the crowd were surrounded by young and old, living

40

or staying either in the houses behind them or in the houses in the uplands – the older men in long jackets thoughtfully smoking their short clay pipes, the womenfolk in jackets and shawls pulling children along by the hand or carrying them in their arms. From out of the frozen ditches which the throng slowly crossed, the pale light of the afternoon sun glinted through the sharp tips of the reeds; it was freezing hard, but the contest pressed forward and every eye constantly followed the flying ball upon which hung the day's honour for the entire village. Each team spokesman carried a white rod with an iron tip – a black one in the case of the uplanders' team – and where the ball came to rest the rod was driven into the hard frozen ground with silent approval or the scornful laughter of the other side, and whoever's ball reached the distant target first would win the contest for his side.

There was little spoken among the crowd; only after a masterly throw would a cheer erupt from the young men or womenfolk; or one of the elderly onlookers would take his pipe out of his mouth, tap the thrower on the shoulder and say a few choice words: "That was a fine throw, said Zacharias, throwing his wife out of the dormer window!" or: "That's how your father used to throw, God bless his soul!" and other such encouraging remarks.

Hauke was unlucky with his first throw: just as he drew back his arm to throw the ball into the air, a cloud shifted from the sun and its full rays shone straight into his eyes; the throw was too short, the ball fell onto a ditch and remained stuck in thin, hollow ice.

"Doesn't count! Doesn't count! Hauke, have another go!" shouted his team mates.

But the spokesman for the uplanders' team quickly disagreed. "It's got to stand – a throw's a throw!"

"Ole! Ole Peters!" shouted the youths from the marsh. "Where is Ole? Where on earth is he?"

But he was already there: "Less of your noise! Well, so Hauke's in trouble? I thought he might be!"

"Rubbish! Hauke's got to throw again. Come on, Ole, show us where your mouth is!"

"It's in the right place!' shouted Ole, striding over to the uplanders' spokesman opposite and coming out with one string of words after another. But gone was the usual sharp, keen thrust of his words. The girl with the dark, closely-knit eyebrows was standing to one side of him, and there was anger in her eyes as she looked at him; but she wasn't allowed a word, for women had no say in the contest.

"You're talking utter rubbish," shouted the other spokesman, "sense just can't get through to you! Sun, moon and stars are all equal to us and firmly set in the heavens; that throw was bungled, and all bungled throws count!"

They continued to argue for some time; but in the end it was the decision of the referee that Hauke could not retake his throw.

"Onwards!" shouted the uplanders, and their spokesman heaved the black rod out of the ground, and the thrower whose number was called took up his position from that spot and threw the ball further. To witness the throw, the dykemaster's head-farmhand had to pass Elke Volkerts: "Who did you leave your wits at home for today then?" she whispered to him.

He glared almost angrily at her, and all traces of humour had disappeared from his broad face. "For you!" he said. "For you've left yours behind too!"

"Go on; I know what you're like, Ole Peters!" retorted the girl, stiffening; but he turned his head away and pretended not to have heard what she had said.

The contest and the black and white rods moved on further. When it was again Hauke's turn to throw, his ball flew so far that the target, a large whitewashed barrel, came clearly into view. He was now a sturdy young fellow who, through his boyhood, had daily studied mathematics and the art of throwing. "Oho, Hauke!" someone shouted from the crowd, "the Archangel Michael himself might have thrown that one!" An old woman with cakes and brandy pushed her way through the crowd towards him; she poured out a full glass and offered it to him. "Come," she said, "let's make up: this is better than the day when you beat my cat to death!" When he looked at her he recognised Trin' Jans. "Thanks, Trin'," he said, "but I don't drink the stuff." He reached into his pocket and pressed a newly-minted one-mark piece into her hand. "Take this, Trin', and drink the glass your-self; then we've made it up!"

"You're right, Hauke!" replied the old woman, as she followed his suggestion; "you're right; and it's better for an old woman like me!"

"How are your ducks?" he called after her as she walked off with her basket; but without turning round she simply shook her head and waved her old hands in the air. "Nothing I can do, Hauke, nothing; there're too many rats in those ditches of yours; the Lord help me; I've got to support myself by other means!" And with that she pushed her way into the midst of the crowd and continued to offer her brandy and honey cakes.

The sun had finally set behind the dyke; in its place a purplish-red glow rose across the sky; occasional black crows flew overhead and were momentarily gilded; evening had come. On the fens, the dark throng of people moved further and further away from the dim shapes of the distant-lying houses and nearer to the barrel; an especially good throw should now be able to reach it. It was the turn of the marshlanders; it was Hauke to throw.

The chalky barrel gleamed white in the lengthening evening shadows that now fell from the dyke over the surface of the frozen pastures. "You'd best leave that one to us!" shouted someone from the uplands, for the contest was now a close one; its team was only ten feet ahead.

The tall, lean figure of the thrower stepped forward from the crowd; the grey eyes in the long Friesian face looked ahead towards the barrel; in one hand, by his side, was the ball.

At that moment he heard the rasping voice of Ole Peters close by his ears: "That bird's too big for you," he said; "do you want us to find you something smaller?"

Hauke swung round and looked him straight in the eyes: "I'm throwing for the marshlanders," he said. "Which side are you on?"

"The same side, I thought, but you're throwing for Elke Volkerts!"

"Get out of my way!" shouted Hauke, preparing himself to throw. But Ole thrust his head even closer. Suddenly, before Hauke himself had a chance to do anything about it, a hand seized Ole and pulled him backwards so that the fellow toppled against his laughing companions. It had not been a large hand that had seized him; for as Hauke swiftly turned his head, he had seen Elke Volkerts beside him straightening her sleeve, her dark eyebrows seeming to express intense anger in her flushed face.

43

The strength of steel flowed into Hauke's arm; he leaned forward a little, weighed the ball a couple of times in his hand; then he swung back his arm, and a deathly silence descended on both sides; every eye followed the flight of the ball, whistling as it cut through the air; suddenly, a good distance from where the ball was thrown, it was hidden by the wings of a herring gull which with a harsh cry flew overhead from the direction of the dyke; at that same moment the noise of the ball striking the barrel could be heard in the distance. "Hurrah for Hauke!" shouted the marshlanders, and noisily the news spread through the crowd: "Hauke! Hauke Haien has won the contest!"

But as the crowd pressed round him, he had reached out to grasp only one hand; and when they shouted again: "What are you waiting for, Hauke, the ball's safely in the barrel!" he just nodded and remained standing where he was; not until he had felt the firm clasp of the small hand in his did he say: "You might be right, I do believe I've won!"

The whole crowd streamed homewards, and Elke and Hauke became separated and carried along by the horde of people on the road to the village inn which wound its way to the uplands round the base of the dykemaster's earthwork. Here, however, they both escaped from the crush, and while Elke went to her room, Hauke remained standing in front of the stable door at the rear of the earthwork watching the dark throng gradually winding its way up to where a room in the village inn stood prepared for the dance. Darkness was gradually descending over the boundless landscape; it grew quieter and quieter around him, only the cattle stirred in the stable behind; from the direction of the uplands he thought he could already hear the piping of clarinets from the inn. Then round the corner of the house he heard the rustle of a dress, and short firm footsteps made their way down the path that led out across the fen to the uplands. Now he saw the figure striding in the twilight, and saw that it was Elke; she too was going to the dance at the inn. The blood rose to his face; shouldn't he run after her and go with her? But Hauke was no hero where women were concerned; occupied with this question, he remained where he was until she disappeared from his sight in the darkness.

Then, when there was no danger of catching her up, he followed the same path until he reached the inn by the church and the babbling and shouting of the people jostling outside and the shrill sound of violins and clarinets filled his ears and deafened him. Unnoticed, he squeezed his way into the "guildroom"; it was not large, and so crowded that it was almost impossible to take one step in front of the other. He went and stood quietly by the doorway and watched the jostling throng; people appeared fools to him; and he had no need to wonder whether anyone was still thinking about the afternoon's contest or about the person who only an hour ago had won it, for every man looked only at his partner and was circling the floor with her. His eyes searched for only one person, and there she was at last – there! She was dancing with her cousin, the young dyke commissioner; but then he saw her no more, only other girls from the marshlands and the uplands who did not interest him. The violins and clarinets suddenly stopped playing and the dance came to an end; but another immediately began. Hauke was struck by the question whether Elke would keep her word, or whether she would dance past him in the arms of Ole Peters. He almost let out a cry at the thought; then – well, what did he want then? But she appeared not to be taking part in this dance, and it finally came to an end, and another, a two-step, that had only just come into fashion here, followed. The music now began to rage. The young lads rushed eagerly for the girls, the candles on the walls flickered. Hauke strained his neck trying to recognise the dancers; and there, one of the third pair, was Ole Peters; but who was his partner? A stocky fellow from the marshlands stood directly in front of her and hid her face! But the dancers moved on and Ole and his partner turned to face him. "Vollina! Vollina Harders!" exclaimed Hauke almost out loud and then sighed with relief. But where was Elke? Didn't she have a partner, or had she refused everyone because she didn't want to dance with Ole? The music stopped again and a new dance began; but still he did not see her. And there was Ole, still dancing with the buxom Vollina in his arms! "Well, well," said Hauke, "it looks as though old Jess Harders with his thirty-seven acres will soon have to go into retirement! – But where is Elke?"

He left his place by the door and pushed further into the room; suddenly he stood before her; she was sitting in a corner with an older friend. "Hauke!" she cried, her fine face looking up at him, "you've come then? But I've not seen you dancing!"

"I haven't been dancing," he replied.

"Why not, Hauke?" and half-rising, she added: "Will you dance with me then? I've refused Ole Peters; he won't be back!"

But Hauke gave no visible response. "Thanks, Elke," he said; "but I'm not very good at it; they might laugh at you, and anyway . . ." He paused suddenly and looked at her tenderly with his grey eyes, as if they were to express the remainder of what he wanted to say.

"What do you mean, Hauke?" she asked softly.

"I mean, Elke, the day couldn't end better for me than it has."

"But of course," she said, "you won the contest."

"Elke!" His admonition could hardly be heard.

Her face suddenly reddened. "Get along with you!" she said, "what do you mean?" and lowered her eyes.

When, however, a lad pulled her friend away to dance, Hauke raised his voice: "I thought, Elke, that I'd won something better!"

Her eyes gazed at the floor for a few moments; then she raised them slowly, and a look, with the quiet strength of her being, met his and flowed through him like warm summer air. "Do as your feelings tell you, Hauke!" she said; "we should know each other well enough by now!"

Elke did not dance again that evening, and when they both set off for home they had clasped each other's hand; in the sky the stars glistened over the silent marsh; a light east wind blew and brought a biting cold; the two of them, however, made for home without cape or cloak, as if spring had suddenly come.

✳ ✳

Hauke had decided on something for which the appropriate occasion, no doubt, would come some time in the future, but out of which he now meant to make a secret celebration for himself. On the following Sunday, accordingly, he went into the town to the old goldsmith Andersen's shop and ordered a solid gold ring. "Show me your finger and we'll measure it!" said the old man, taking hold of his ring finger. "Well," he said, "it's not as thick as usual with you folk!" But Hauke replied: "Measure the little finger," and held it out.

The goldsmith looked at him slightly puzzled; but what did he care about the whims of young farming lads? "I think there'll be something more suitable among the girls' rings!" he said, and Hauke felt the blood rise in both his cheeks. But the small gold ring fitted his little finger, and he took it hastily and paid for it in silver; then with a pounding heart he slipped it into his waistcoat pocket as if he were performing a ceremonial act.

He carried it on his person every day from that moment on, uneasily but proudly, as if the waistcoat pocket were only there for the purpose of carrying a ring. So he carried it for many a day and year; the ring even had to be moved into a new waistcoat pocket; the occasion to take it out had still not come. It had indeed crossed his mind to go straight to the dykemaster, for his father after all was a respected member of the village community. But in a calmer moment he knew very well that the old dykemaster would simply have laughed his farmhand out of court. So he and the dykemaster's daughter continued to live in each other's company; she in girlish silence, yet both as if they were at all times close to each other.

A year after that winter's contest Ole Peters gave in his notice and married Vollina Harders. Hauke had been right; her father had retired, and instead of the buxom daughter the lively son-in-law now rode the light-brown mare over the fen, and always on his return, it was said, rode it along the side of the dyke. Hauke had become the head-farmhand and a younger lad had taken his old place. The dykemaster had resisted promoting him at first: "Farmhand's better!" he had growled; "I need him here where my books are!" But Elke had remonstrated with him: "Then you'll lose Hauke too, father!" and the old man had grown afraid. Hauke got his promotion, but continued just as before to help the dykemaster with his work.

After a further year, however, Hauke began to discuss his personal situation with Elke. His father's health was failing and the few summer days that the dykemaster allowed him to work on his father's land were no longer enough; his father was struggling and he could no longer bear to look on. – It was a summer's evening; the couple stood in the twilight under the mighty ash tree in front of the door. The girl stared silently for a while up at the branches of the tree; then she said: "I haven't wanted to say anything just yet, Hauke; I thought you'd do what was right."

"Then I must leave your house," he said, "and not come back."

They were silent for a moment and gazed at the setting sun sinking slowly into the sea beyond the dyke. "You must know," she said; "I was with your father this morning and found him asleep in his armchair with his sketching pen in his hand and the drawing board with a half-finished drawing on it on the table in front of him. When he woke up he chatted to me for about a quarter of an hour, with some difficulty, and when I wanted to go he anxiously held me back by the hand as if he was afraid that it might be for the last time; but . . ."

"But what, Elke?" asked Hauke, as she faltered.

Tears ran down the girl's cheeks. "I was only thinking of my father," she said; "believe me, it will be hard on him without you." And as if she had to summon up courage for the remaining words, she added: "I often have the feeling he's preparing for his deathbed."

Hauke did not answer; he suddenly felt as if the ring stirred in his pocket; but even before he had suppressed his annoyance at this instinctive reaction, Elke continued: "No, don't feel angry, Hauke! I know you won't abandon us!"

Eagerly he seized her hand, and she did not withdraw it. The young couple continued to stand together for a while in the gathering darkness until their hands finally slipped apart and they each went their separate ways. A sudden gust of wind swept through the leaves of the ash tree and rattled the shutters at the front of the house; gradually night came and silence lay over the vast landscape.

Through Elke's intervention Hauke had been relieved of his duties by the old dykemaster without the need to give the required period of notice, and two new farmhands were now in the house. A few months later Tede Haien died; but before he died he called his son to his bedside. "Sit close to me, my child," said the old man in a weak voice, "close to me! Don't be afraid; there's only the angel of death here – come to call me away."

48

And the distressed son sat down close by the dark wall-bed: "What is it you want to say, father?"

"There is something, my son," said the old man and stretched his hands across the bed covering. "When you were only a youngster and went to work for the dykemaster, you took it into your head that you would be dykemaster yourself one day. That made an impression on me, and gradually I also came to think that you were the right man for the job. But your inheritance for such a post was too small – I've lived frugally while you've been at work – I thought I'd increase it for you."

Hauke grasped his father's hands passionately, and the old man struggled to raise himself to see him. "Yes, yes, my son," he said, "the document's there in the top drawer of the strongbox. As you know, old Antje Wohlers has a fen of about eight acres; in her crippled old age, though, she couldn't live off it; so for some time now, around Martinmas, I've been paying the poor old soul a regular sum, and more when I could afford it, and for that she's transferred the land to me; it's all legally in order. – Now she's dying too: the sickness of these parts, cancer, has finally caught up with her; you won't need to make any more payments to her!"

He closed his eyes for a while; then he continued: "It's not much, I know; but it's more than you had while you were here with me. May it serve you well in your days on earth!"

During his son's words of gratitude, the old man fell asleep. He had nothing more to attend to; and a few days later the angel of death came to close his eyes for good, and Hauke inherited his father's estate.

The day after the funeral Elke visited his house. "It's good of you to look in, Elke!" said Hauke, by way of greeting her.

But she replied: "I'm not just looking in; I've come to tidy up a bit so that you can live decently in your home! Your father was always too wrapped up in his sketches and figures to notice things, and death makes disorder worse; I'll make the place livable again for you!"

He looked at her, his grey eyes full of trust: "Tidy up then!" he said; "I like it that way too."

And then she began to tidy up: the drawing board that still lay there was dusted off and taken to the loft, the drawing pens, pencil and chalk were carefully put away in the drawer of the strongbox; a young servant girl was then called to help and all the furniture in the living room was repositioned so that the room appeared brighter and larger. "Only we women can do that!" smiled Elke. Hauke, in spite of the grief for his father, had looked on with a gleam of pleasure in his eyes, helping too when necessary.

And when towards dusk – it was now early September – everything was as she wanted it to be for him, she seized his hand and beckoned to him with her dark eyes: "Now come and eat with us this evening; I had to promise father to bring you back with me; when you then go home, you'll have nothing to worry about, your house will be ready!"

When they entered the dykemaster's spacious living room, where because the windows were shuttered both the candles on the table were lit, he made to get up out of his armchair but, sinking back under his own heavy weight, called out instead to his former farmhand: "It's right, it's right, Hauke, that you should keep in touch with your old friends! Only come a bit nearer, nearer still!" And when Hauke reached his chair he seized him with chubby hands. "Well, well, my lad," he said, "don't take it to heart, we all have to die sometime, and your father wasn't among the hindmost! – Elke, see to it now that the roast is on the table; we must keep our strength up! There's work for us to do, Hauke! The autumn inspection's approaching; there's the dyke and sluice accounts piled high, the recent damage to the dyke at Westerkoog – I don't know how to keep this old head of mine above water, but you've got a much younger one on your shoulders, thank God; you're a good lad, Hauke!"

After this long speech in which he had poured out his heart, the old man sank back into his armchair and blinked longingly towards the doorway through which Elke was just appearing with the roast. Hauke stood smiling beside him. "Take a seat," said the dykemaster, "so we shan't waste too much time; when it's cold it doesn't taste so good!"

And Hauke sat down at the table; it seemed quite natural for him to share Elke's father's work. And when the autumn inspection had come and gone and a few more moons had passed, he had certainly done the greater part of it.'

The narrator paused and looked around. A gull's cry sounded against the window, and the stamping of feet could be heard in the hallway outside the guests' room, as if someone were trying to remove the clay from his heavy boots.

The dykemaster and the members of the dyke committee turned their heads towards the door. 'What's up?' shouted the dykemaster.

A burly man, a sou'wester on his head, entered the room. 'Sir,' he said, 'we both saw it, Hans Nickels and myself: the rider on the grey – plunged into the pond!'

'Where did you see it?' asked the dykemaster.

'There's only one breach pond, in Jansen's fen, where the Hauke Haien Polder begins.'

'You saw it just the once?'

'Only the once, sir; it was only like a shadow; but that doesn't mean it was the first time.'

The dykemaster had stood up. 'You'll have to excuse us,' he said, turning to me, 'we need to go outside to see where the danger threatens!' Then he went out of the door with the messenger, and the rest of the company followed him.

I remained alone with the schoolmaster in the large deserted guests' room; through the uncurtained windows, no longer hidden by the backs of the guests, there was now a clear view of the storm driving the dark clouds across the sky.

The old man remained seated at the table, a superior, yet sympathetic smile on his lips. 'It's become too empty in here,' he said; 'may I invite you up to my room? I live here in this house; and believe me, I am well acqainted with the weather on the dykes; there's nothing we need be afraid of.'

I thankfully accepted his invitation for I was beginning to shiver, and accompanied by the flame of a candle we climbed the stairs to a room in the attic which also faced west, but here the windows were hung with dark woollen curtains. In a bookcase I saw a modest collection of books, and next to it the portraits of two elderly professors; in front of a table stood a large wing chair. 'Make yourself comfortable!' said my friendly host and threw some peat into a small still-glowing stove the top of which was crowned by a tin kettle. 'Won't be long! It will soon be whistling; then I'll brew us a tumbler of grog – that'll keep you awake!'

'I don't need that,' I said; 'I don't feel at all sleepy when I accompany your Hauke on his life's journey!'

'Really?' he said, gesturing in my direction with his intelligent eyes after I had comfortably settled into his armchair. 'Where were we then? – Oh yes; I know! So then:

Hauke had inherited his father's property, and as old Antje Wohlers had also succumbed to her suffering, her fenland had been added to it. But since the death, or more precisely, since the last words of his father, something had grown inside him whose seed he had carried since early boyhood; all too frequently he repeated to himself that he was the right man if a new dykemaster were to be needed. That was it; his father, who was bound to understand it, and who had most certainly been the most intelligent man in the village, had added these words like a last gift to him as part of his inheritance: the Wohlers' fenland, for which he also had to thank him, was to form the first stepping-stone on the way to that height! For indeed, even with all his father's fenland, a dykemaster still had to be able to show that he owned even more land! – But his father had lived frugally in those lonely years, and with what he had denied himself he had bought the new property; he too could do that, he could do more; for his father's strength had already been used up, but he could do the hardest work for years on end! – Yet it had to be said that even if he were to succeed in meeting a dykemaster's requirements on this score, the sharp edge that he had added to the old dykemaster's administration had made him no friendships in the village, whereas Ole Peters, his old adversary, had recently been left a legacy and was beginning to become a wealthy man. A sea of faces came flooding into his mind and they all looked at him with hostile eyes; then resentment against these people seized him: he stretched out his arm as though to grab them, for they wanted to push him from an office only he of all of them was fitted to hold. – And these thoughts never left him; they were again and again with him, and so within his young soul there grew up alongside uprightness and love also ambition and hatred. But these he locked away deep within himself; not even Elke had any idea they were there.

There was a wedding when the new year came; the bride was a relative of the Haiens, and Hauke and Elke were both there as invited guests; indeed, at the meal, because a close relative failed to turn up, they found themselves sitting next to each other; only a fleeting smile across both their faces betrayed their delight. But today Elke sat indifferent to the chatting and clinking of glasses around her.

"Is something wrong?" asked Hauke.

"Oh, not really; there're just too many people here for me, that's all."

"But you look so sad!"

She shook her head; then they did not speak again.

Her silence aroused a surge of something like jealousy within him, and discreetly he clasped her hand under the overhanging tablecloth; but she did not start away, her hand met trustingly with his. Had she been overcome by loneliness now that she had to witness the declining figure of her father every day? Hauke did not think to ask himself this question; but his breath stood still as he took the gold ring from his pocket. "Will you wear this for me?" he said trembling, while he slipped the ring onto the finger of her slender hand.

The pastor's wife sat opposite at the same table; she suddenly laid down her fork and turned to her neighbour: "My God, the girl!" she cried; "she's gone deathly white!"

But the blood soon returned to Elke's face. "Can you wait, Hauke?" she asked softly.

The shrewd Friesian pondered for a few moments, then said: "Wait for what?"

"You know; I don't have to tell you."

"Of course not," he said; "yes, Elke, I can wait – if only there were an end in sight!"

"O God, I'm afraid, so close! Don't speak like that, Hauke; you're talking about my father's death!" She laid her other hand on her breast: "Until then," she said, "I shall carry the gold ring here; you've no need to fear that I shall return it during my lifetime!"

They both smiled and squeezed each other's hands so hard that on any other occasion the girl would have cried out.

The pastor's wife, meanwhile, had been constantly scrutinising

53

Elke's eyes which under the lace quilling of a gold brocade cap were glowing like embers in a dark fire. Amid the growing din at the table, however, she had not understood anything; nor did she turn to her neighbour, because a prospective marriage such as the one that appeared to be developing here in front of her – if only because of the ensuing marriage fees eventually coming to her husband, the pastor – she did not care to endanger.

❊ ❊

Elke's premonition was fulfilled; one morning after Easter the dykemaster, Tede Volkerts, had been found dead in his bed; his face showed that the end had been a peaceful one. In the last few months he had repeatedly expressed a weariness with life; his favourite dish, his roast, even his ducks were no longer to his taste.

There was now a grand funeral in the village. In the uplands, on the western side of the cemetery that surrounded the church, was a well-kept family grave enclosed within wrought-iron railings; leaning against a weeping ash stood a wide blue gravestone on which a death's head with strong toothy jaws had been carved; beneath it, in capital letters, the inscription:

> THIS IS DEATH WHO DEVOURS US ALL –
> WISDOM AND KNOWLEDGE HE TAKES AWAY.
> A WISE MAN HERE HAS HEARD DEATH'S CALL –
> GOD GRANT HIM A BLESSED JUDGMENT DAY.

This was the resting place of the previous dykemaster, Volkert Tedsen; a fresh grave had been dug in which his son, the just deceased dykemaster, Tede Volkerts, would shortly be buried. And the funeral procession was already emerging from the marshland below, a collection of wagons from all the villages in the parish; the heavy coffin rested on the leading wagon which was already being hauled up the sandy slope towards the uplands by two shiny black horses from the dykemaster's own stable; the horses' tails and manes blew in the strong spring wind. The cemetery round the church was filled to its boundary with people; boys with small children in their arms were even squatting on top of the stone portal. They all wanted to see the burial.

At the farmstead below in the marshland Elke had prepared the funeral supper in the guest and living rooms; vintage wine had been put beside each place; beside the chief dykemaster's – for he too was present today – and the pastor's a bottle of Langkork each. When everything had been attended to, Elke went out through the stable to the farm entrance; she met no one on the way; the farmhands were with the two teams of horses in the funeral procession. At the gate she stopped and, her dark mourning clothes fluttering in the spring wind, watched the last of the wagons moving through the village up the hill towards the church. After a while there was a burst of activity that seemed to be followed by a deathly hush. Elke folded her hands; now they were probably lowering the coffin into the grave: ". . . for dust thou art, and unto dust shalt thou return!" Involuntarily, quietly, as if she could hear it from where she stood, she repeated the words; then her eyes filled with tears, and hands, folded across her breast, sank slowly to her lap: "Our Father, which art in heaven!" she fervently prayed. And at the end of the Lord's Prayer she remained standing, motionless, for a long time, she the present owner of this large marshland farmstead; and thoughts of life and death rose in conflict within her.

A distant rumbling roused her. When she opened her eyes she saw the wagons again, one after the other, moving swiftly down across the marsh and closer and closer to her farmstead. She straightened herself up, gave a sharp look around her once more, then returned the way she had come, back through the stable and into the ceremonially prepared living rooms. No one was here either; only through the wall could she hear the sound of the maids bustling about the kitchen. The tables for the funeral supper stood still and deserted; the mirror between the windows was covered with white sheets as were the brass knobs on the heating stove; nothing now glinted in the room. Elke saw that the doors of the wall-bed, in which her father had slept for the last time, were open and she went over and closed them firmly together; without thinking she read the short epigram written on them in gold letters between roses and carnations:

WHEN DAILY WORK IS RIGHTLY DONE,
THEN HONEST SLEEP IS JUSTLY WON.

That was from grandfather's days! – She glanced at the wall cabinet; it was almost empty, but through the glass doors she could still see the polished goblet which, as her father used to be so fond of relating, had once been awarded to him in his youth as a prize in a riding tournament. She took it out of the cabinet and placed it beside the chief dykemaster's place at the table. Then she went to the window, as she could already hear the wagons coming up the earthwork towards the farmhouse; one after the other stopped in front of the house, and the guests, more lively than when they had first come, jumped down from their seats. Rubbing their hands and chatting, they all pressed their way forward into the room and it was not long before everybody was seated at the arranged table upon which steamed well-prepared food; the chief dykemaster sat with the pastor in the guest room, and the noise and loud chatter soon spread along the table as if death's terrible stillness had never settled here. Quietly, eyes only on her guests, Elke went round the tables with her maids, ensuring that nothing was found wanting at the meal. Even Hauke Haien sat in the living room next to Ole Peters and other minor landowners.

After the meal had ended the white clay pipes were fetched from the corner and lit and Elke was again busy offering cups of coffee to all the guests; for even here no expense was being spared. In the living room by the deceased's desk, the chief dyke-master stood in conversation with the pastor and the white-haired dyke commissioner, Jewe Manners. "It went well, gentlemen," said the chief dykemaster, "we've laid the old dykemaster honourably to rest; but where's the new one coming from? I think you'll need to take over this post, Manners!"

Smiling, the elderly Manners lifted the black velvet cap from his white hair: "Chief Dykemaster," he said, "the game wouldn't last long enough; when the late Tede Volkerts became dykemaster, I became commissioner and I've been in that post now for a good forty years!"

"That's no handicap, Manners; you'll know the job even better, and have no trouble with it!"

But the old man shook his head: "No, no, Your Honour. Leave me where I am, I can go on for a few more years yet!"

The pastor supported him: "Why not," he said, "give the job to the person who has actually been doing it for the last few years?"

The chief dykemaster looked at him: "I don't understand, pastor!"

But the pastor pointed his finger at the guest room where Hauke appeared to be explaining something slowly and carefully to two elderly people. "The one standing there," he said; "the tall Friesian with the intelligent grey eyes and the lean nose and prominent forehead! He was the old man's farmhand but now manages his own small farm; it's true, though, he is rather young!"

"Looks in his thirties," said the chief dykemaster, examining the man who had been described to him.

"He's not yet twenty-four," observed Commissioner Manners; "but the pastor's quite right: everything of value to the dykes, sluices and such like that was proposed by the dykemaster's office in the last few years came from him; towards the end the old man was quite beyond it."

"Indeed, indeed?" mused the chief dykemaster; "and in your opinion he would be just the man now to move into his master's old job?"

"He would certainly be the right man," responded Jewe Manners; "but he lacks what people here call 'clay under his feet'; his father had about twenty-two acres of land – Hauke might well now have a good thirty – but no one here has ever become dykemaster with as little land as that."

The pastor was just about to open his mouth, as if to raise a slight objection, when Elke Volkerts who had been in the room for some time suddenly walked up to them. "Would you allow me a word, Your Honour?" she said to the high official; "it is just so that an error is not turned into a wrong!"

"Of course, Fräulein Elke!" he replied; "wisdom from the lips of a beautiful girl is always worth hearing!"

"It's not wisdom, Your Honour; I just want to speak the truth."

"That, too, needs to be heard, Fräulein Elke!"

The girl's dark eyes glanced to one side for a moment, as though to avoid being overheard by extra pairs of ears: "Your Honour," she began, breathing heavily, "my godfather, Jewe Manners, said to you that Hauke Haien owned only about thirty acres of land; that is perfectly true at the moment, but as soon as is right, Hauke will have as many more acres to call his own as this farmstead, my father's, now mine; taken altogether he will have more than sufficient for a dykemaster."

The aged Manners craned his white head towards her as though he first had to see who was actually talking: "What's all this?" he said; "what are you talking about, child?"

But Elke pulled a shiny gold ring on a black ribbon from her bodice: "I'm engaged, godfather," she said; "here's the ring, and Hauke Haien is my fiancé."

"And when – I am allowed to ask as I am your godfather, Elke Volkerts – when did this happen?"

"It was some considerable time ago; but I was of age, godfather," she said; "my father was already old and feeble, and knowing him as I did, I didn't want to trouble him with such things; now that he's with God he will understand that his child is in safe hands with this man. I wouldn't have mentioned it throughout the year of mourning; but now, for the sake of Hauke and for the sake of the polder, I had to speak out about it." And facing the chief dykemaster, she continued: "Your Honour will pardon me for doing so!"

The three men looked at one another; the pastor laughed, the aged commissioner digested it with a "H'm, h'm!" while the chief dykemaster, as though he were about to make an important decision, rubbed his brow. "Of course, my dear young lady," he said finally, "but how then does the law stand here in the polder concerning property rights after marriage? I must confess, I'm not entirely versed in such complex matters!"

"Your Honour has no need to be," replied the dykemaster's daughter, "I shall transfer the land to my fiancé before the marriage. I too have my small pride," she continued with a smile; "I want to marry the richest man in the village!"

"Now, Manners," observed the pastor, "I think that you as her godfather would not have any objection if I were to join the new dykemaster to the old one's daughter in marriage!"

The old commissioner gently shook his head: "May the Lord give his blessing," he said reverently.

The chief dykemaster, however, offered the girl his hand. "You've spoken truthfully and wisely, Elke Volkerts; I thank you for such a forthright contribution, and I also hope in the future, and under less tragic circumstances than today's, to be a guest in your home; but – for a dykemaster to be created by such a young lady as yourself – well now, that's really astonishing!"

"Your Honour," replied Elke, once again looking at the kindly chief official with her serious eyes, "even a woman is surely allowed to help the right man!" Then she went into the adjoining guest room and in silence laid her hand in Hauke Haien's.

✽ ✽

It was some years later: a hard-working labourer and his wife and child now occupied Tede Haien's small house; the young dykemaster lived with his wife, Elke Volkerts, on her father's farm. In summer the mighty ash rustled as usual in front of the house; but on the bench that now stood beneath it, mostly only the young wife was to be seen in the evenings, alone with some household task in hand; the marriage was still childless; the husband had other things to do than sit out in front of his door in the evenings, for despite the work that he had put in for the old dykemaster, many unfinished tasks remained from his administration, tasks which at the time Hauke had not deemed it prudent to tackle; but now everything had to be dealt with progressively and he made a clean sweep of them all. On top of this came the management of his own farm, extended from the land he had previously owned, a task in which he was still trying to save hiring a farmhand. The married couple, therefore, apart from Sundays when they went to church, saw each other mostly at a midday lunch hastily prepared by Hauke and at the beginning and end of the day; it was a life of unremitting toil, yet a satisfying one nevertheless.

Then a disturbing remark began to circulate. – It was one Sunday after church when a somewhat unruly crowd of young landowners from the marsh and the uplands had stayed behind in the village inn to have a few drinks, and were talking over a fourth or fifth glass, not, it must be said, about the king or the government – such lofty matters were not raised at that time – but about municipal officers and high officials, above all about the local taxes and charges, and the more they talked the less good they found to say about any of them, especially the new dyke charges; all the dyke and polder sluices, which up until then had always been in working order, were now being found in need of repair; on the dykes, they complained, new faults were always being discovered that needed hundreds of barrow-loads of earth; to the devil with the lot of it!

"All this stems from your clever dykemaster," shouted one of the uplanders, "who always goes about brooding and pokes his nose into every damn thing!"

"Yes, Marten," said Ole Peters, who was sitting opposite the speaker; "you're right, he's underhand, that one, and spends all his time trying to impress the chief dykemaster – but we're saddled with him!"

"Why did you let him be foisted on you?" said the other; "you're paying for it now."

Ole Peters laughed. "Yes, Marten Fedders, but that's how things are now, and they can't be changed; the old man became dykemaster on account of his father, the new one on account of his wife!" The laughter that ran round the table showed how well this remark was received.

It had been said at a public table at the inn and it did not remain there, it soon spread throughout the uplands – and through the village below in the marshland; and it reached Hauke too. Once more the sea of leering faces came flooding into his mind, and even more scornful than it had actually been, he could hear their laughter at the table at the inn. "Dogs!" he cried, and he looked around him furiously as though he wanted to have them whipped.

Elke placed her hand on his arm: "Don't let them worry you; they'd all love to be what you are!"

"That's just it!" he replied resentfully.

"And anyway," she continued, "hasn't Ole Peters married into property himself?"

"That might be so, Elke; but what he gained from Vollina didn't add up to being a dykemaster!"

"Best to say *he* didn't add up to being one!" and Elke turned her husband round so that he had to see himself in the mirror, for they were both standing between the windows of their bedroom. "There stands the dykemaster!" she said; "now take a good look at him; only those fit for office should hold it!"

"What you're saying is not wrong," he replied thoughtfully, "but then . . . Now, Elke; I must have a look at the east sluice, the gates aren't shutting properly again!"

She pressed his hand: "Come, look at me just for once! What's the matter? Your eyes are looking so far away!"

"Nothing, Elke, you're quite right."

He left; but it was not long before the repairs to the sluice were forgotten. A quite different idea seized hold of him, something he had only partially thought through and had carried about with him for many a year but which had been submerged beneath the pressing duties of his office, and now it took possession of his thoughts again, more powerful than ever before, as if it had suddenly sprouted wings.

Scarcely knowing how he came to be there, he found himself on top of the main dyke and already quite a way south towards the town; the village on his left, which lay to this side of it, had long since vanished from sight; still he strode on, his eyes constantly trained seaward towards the wide expanse of foreland; anyone who might have been with him would not have failed to notice the intense mental activity going on behind those eyes. Finally he stopped: the foreland here narrowed to a thin strip of land that ran next to the dyke. "It must be," he said to himself. "Seven years in office; they shall not say again that I'm only dyke-master because of my wife!"

He continued to stand there, his eyes sharply and carefully scanning the length and breadth of the green foreland; then he walked back to a point where the broad expanse of land that lay before him again reduced to a narrow strip of green pasture. Cutting through it, however, and running hard along the length of the dyke, was a fast flowing stream of water which virtually separated the whole foreland from the mainland and turned it into a hallig; it was spanned by a crude wooden bridge over which livestock, haywains and cornwagons could get across and back. It was low tide, and the gold September sun sparkled on the strip of mud which was almost a hundred paces wide and on the deep watercourse in the middle of it along which, even now, the sea still drove its waters. "That can be dammed!" said Hauke to himself, after contemplating the scene for some time; then he looked up, and from the dyke on which he stood drew in his mind, beyond the watercourse, a line round the detached area of land, first in an arc southwards, then eastwards over the continuing watercourse there, and finally back up to the dyke.

The line he had just drawn was of a new dyke, new also in its form, which until this moment had existed only in his mind.

"That would produce a polder of about fifteen hundred acres," he said smiling to himself; "not exactly huge; but . . ."

Another calculation occupied his thoughts: the foreland belonged to the community here, shared out among its individual members according to their property-holding within the district, or acquired by some other legal means; he began to count up how many shares he had acquired from his father, how many from Elke's father, and how many he had bought during his marriage, partly with a vague hope of future profit and partly to develop his sheep breeding business. It was already an impressive amount; for he had also bought Ole Peters' entire holding when he was devastated by the loss of his best ram during a flood. But that had been an unusual incident, for as long as Hauke could remember only the edges of the foreland were ever flooded even at high tide levels. What excellent pasture and cornfields there would be, and of what value, when it was all enclosed by his new dyke! He was drunk with the thought of it; but he pressed his nails into the palms of his hands and forced his eyes to see clearly and soberly what lay before him: a huge dykeless area, exposed to who knows what storms and floods in the coming years, along whose outermost edge a flock of dirty-looking sheep now grazed; a mountain of additional work for him, struggle and trouble! But for all that, as he made his way down from the dyke and along the path across the fens towards his farmstead, it was as if he carried home with him a priceless treasure.

Elke came towards him in the hall. "How was the sluice?" she asked.

He looked down at her with a mysterious smile: "We'll soon be needing another one," he said, "and new dyke sluices, and a new dyke!"

"I don't understand you," replied Elke, as they went into the room; "what is it you want to do, Hauke?"

"I want," he said slowly and then paused for a moment, "I want to dyke that large expanse of foreland that starts opposite our farmstead and extends out to the west, and make it into a good sound polder: the flood tides have left us in peace for almost a lifetime; but if a bad one comes again and destroys the growth there, at one fell swoop the whole precious lot will be lost for ever; only the old lax management has let it stay like that till now!"

She looked at him in amazement. "And you blame yourself and no one else?" she said.

"I do, Elke; but until now there have been too many other things to do!"

"Of course, Hauke; you've certainly done enough!"

He had seated himself in the old dykemaster's armchair, and both his hands firmly gripped its rests.

"Have you really the stomach for it, Hauke?" his wife asked him.

"I have, Elke!" he responded quickly.

"Don't be hasty, Hauke; it will be perilous work; and nearly everyone will be against you – no one will ever thank you for your worry and trouble!"

He nodded: "I know!" he said.

"And if it were to go wrong?" she asked again. "Ever since I was a child I have heard that the watercourse cannot be blocked, and for that reason should never be touched."

"That was a lazy man's excuse!" said Hauke; "why shouldn't it be possible to block the watercourse?"

"I never heard why; perhaps because it flows straight to the sea; the current's too strong." – Something flashed through her mind, and an almost mischievous sparkle appeared in her serious eyes: "When I was a child," she said, "I once heard the farmhands over there talking about it: they said that for a dyke to hold there, something living had to be thrown into it while it was being built. During the building of a dyke on the other side, a good hundred years ago, they said that a gypsy's baby was thrown into it which the mother had been persuaded to sell for a small fortune; but no one would sell their child today!"

Hauke shook his head. "Then it's good we haven't got one, they'd be sure to demand it from us!"

"They wouldn't get it!" cried Elke and threw her arms around her body as though afraid.

Hauke smiled; but she asked again: "And the enormous costs? Have you considered those?"

"I have, Elke; the money we can make will much more than recover the expense, even the maintenance costs of the old dyke will be largely covered by the new one; we'll join in the work our-selves and there are over eighty teams of horses and wagons in the district we can call on; there's no shortage of young muscle around here either. At least you won't have made me dykemaster for nothing, Elke; I'll show them that I am a real dykemaster!"

She had squatted down in front of him, looking at him anxiously; she now raised herself with a sigh: "I must get on with my day's work," she said, and she brushed her hand slowly over his cheek; "you do yours, Hauke!"

"Amen, Elke!" he said with a serious smile. "There's work for us both!"

And there was indeed work enough for them both, but the heavier load now fell onto the husband's shoulders. On Sunday afternoons, and often after work, Hauke would sit with a capa-ble surveyor deeply engrossed in mathematical problems, draw-ings and outline plans. If he was alone it was just the same and the work often was not finished until well after midnight when he would creep softly into the bedroom – for the stifling wall-beds in the living room were no longer used in Hauke's household – and his wife, so that he might finally get some rest, would lie with her eyes closed, feigning sleep, although she had waited up for him with a pounding heart; then sometimes he would kiss her on the forehead and murmur a loving word or two before settling him-self down to a sleep that seldom came before the first cock-crow. In a winter storm he would run out onto the dyke, paper and pencil in hand, and stand and draw and take notes while a gust of wind ripped the cap from his head and his long fair hair flew about his flushed face; soon, if the boat's passage was not obstructed by ice, he and a farmhand would be out in a boat in the shallows, with plumb-line and rod, measuring the depths of the currents, about which he was still unsure. Elke often trembled with fear for him; but once he was back again he would only be able to notice it by the firm grasp of her hand or by the radiant flash in her usually calm eyes. "Patience, Elke," he said once, when it seemed to him that his wife would not let him go; "I've got to be sure about this myself first, before I submit my propos-al." She nodded and let him go. The number of rides to the town to see the chief dykemaster did not reduce either, and all this piled on top of the concerns of the farm and the estate was followed by further work well into the night. Hauke's association with other people, except through work and business, all but ceased; even his wife he saw less and less. "These are bad times, and they're going to go on for a long time yet," said Elke to herself, and she went on with her work.

At last the spring winds and the sun had broken up the ice everywhere, and all the preparatory work was done; the application to the chief dykemaster for recommendation to higher authority – containing a proposal for the dyking of the foreland for the benefit of the people, and especially of the old polder, and not least the Royal Treasury which, within a few short years, would benefit from the taxes arising from about fifteen hundred acres – had been neatly copied out and, together with enclosed outline plans and drawings of the coastal regions present and future and of the polder and dyke sluices, and everything else that concerned the proposal, rolled up into a bundle and stamped with the dykemaster's official seal.

"That's it, Elke," said the young dykemaster, "now come and give it your blessing!"

Elke laid her hand in his. "We must stand firmly together," she said.

"We will."

❧ ❧

Then the application was delivered to the town by mounted messenger.

– You will be aware, my dear sir,' said the schoolmaster, interrupting his story, his keen eyes gazing at me in a friendly way, 'that what I've told you so far has been gathered during my almost forty years of service here in this polder from accounts of rational people, or from the reminiscences of their grandchildren and great-grandchildren; what I now have to lay before you, however, so that you can relate all this to its final outcome, was at the time, and still is even today, the gossip of the entire village here in the marsh as soon as the spinning wheels start to whirr around All Saints' Day.

From the ridge of the dyke, some five to six hundred paces

northwards from the dykemaster's farmstead, a few thousand paces out across the shallows and somewhat further away from the shore of the marsh opposite, a small hallig which people called "Jeverssand", also "Jevershallig", could be seen at that time. It had still been used by the grandfathers of those days for sheep-grazing, since grass had grown there until recently; but even that had now ceased because the low hallig had been submerged by the sea a few times, in high summer too, which had stunted its growth and made it unsuitable for sheep-grazing. So it came about that the hallig's only visitors were gulls and other birds that fly along the shore, including occasional osprey; and from the dyke on moonlit evenings only thick or thin blankets of fog could be seen drifting over it. A few bleached bones of drowned sheep and the skeleton of a horse – no one quite understood how that came to be there – were also claimed to be recognisable when the moon shone on the hallig from the east.

It was towards the end of March, in the evening after work, when the day-labourer from Tede Haien's farm and Iven Johns, the young dykemaster's farmhand, stood motionless together at this spot on the dyke and stared across at the hallig that was barely visible in the hazy moonlight; something startling appeared to be keeping them there. The day-labourer stuck his hands into his pockets and shrugged his shoulders: "Come on, Iven," he said, "I don't like this at all; let's go home!"

The other laughed, even though there was a touch of fear in his voice: "Nonsense, it's a live creature, a big one! Who the devil chased it out there onto that stretch of mud? Now look, it's stretching its neck towards us! No, it's lowering its head, it's grazing! I would've thought there was no grazing over there! What on earth can it be?"

"It's nothing to do with us!" replied the other. "Good night, Iven, if you're not coming, I'm going home!"

"It's all right for you, you've got a wife and a warm bed to go to! There's only the cold March air in my bedroom!"

"Good night then!" the labourer called back as he trudged home along the dyke. The farmhand stood for a while watching his companion go; but the fascination of the eerie sight held him rooted to the spot. Then a dark, stocky figure came towards him along the dyke from the direction of the village; it was the dykemaster's servant boy. "What do you want, Carsten?" the farmhand called out to him.

"Me? – nothing," said the boy. "But the master wants to speak with you, Iven Johns!"

The farmhand's gaze was fixed again on the hallig: "Right away. I'm coming right away!" he said.

"What on earth are you staring at?" asked the boy.

The farmhand raised his arm and pointed silently towards the hallig. "Heh!" whispered the boy, "there's a horse moving over there – a grey – it's got to be the devil's – however did a horse come to be on Jevershallig?"

"Don't know, Carsten; assuming it's a real horse, that is!"

"Of course it is, Iven. Just look, it's grazing just like a horse! But who took it there? We don't have a boat big enough in the village! Maybe it's just a sheep; Peter Ohm says that by moonlight even ten peat circles look like a whole village. Now look! It's rearing up – it must be a horse!"

They both stood awhile in silence, their eyes focused only on whatever it was they could see moving dimly before them. The moon was at its height and lit up the vast tidal flats across which the rising waters of the tide had begun to cover the glittering surfaces of the mud. Only the gentle sound of the water, no cry of animal or bird, was to be heard here in the immense space; even the marsh behind the dyke was deserted; the cows and the bulls were long since returned to the stalls. Nothing stirred; only what they thought to be a horse, a grey, appeared to be still moving out there on Jevershallig. "It's getting lighter," said the farmhand, breaking the silence. "I can clearly see the white skeletons of the sheep glinting!"

"So can I," said the boy, craning his neck; then, as if it had suddenly occurred to him, he tugged at the farmhand's sleeve. "Iven," he whispered, "that horse's skeleton out there – where is it? I can't see it!"

"I can't see it either – strange!" said the farmhand.

"Not so strange, Iven! Sometimes, I'm not sure which nights, the bones are supposed to rise up and act as if they were alive!"

"Really?" said Iven. "That's just old women's talk!"

"Could be, Iven," said the boy.

"I thought you came to fetch me. Come on, we'd better be off home! Nothing much happening here."

The boy would not be moved, however, until the farmhand had forcibly turned him round and marched him on his way. "Listen, Carsten," said Iven, when the ghostly hallig was a good way behind, "you're a lad who's game for anything; I'm sure you'd love to go and explore that place yourself!"

"Yes," replied Carsten, still trembling slightly. "Yes, I would, Iven!"

"You're quite serious?" said Iven, after the boy had insisted on shaking hands on it. "Then we'll cast off our boat tomorrow night; you row out to Jevershallig, I'll stay and wait for you on the dyke."

"All right," replied the boy, "that'll be fine! I'll take my whip along!"

"Yes, do!"

After a slow climb up the high earthwork, they arrived in silence at the dykemaster's farmstead.

❈ ❈

At about the same time on the following evening the farmhand was sitting on the large stone in front of the stable door when the servant boy came towards him cracking his whip. "That's a strange sound for a whip!" said the former.

"It is, watch out," replied the boy; "I've attached some nails to the cord."

"Let's be off," said Iven.

The moon, as on the previous day, was high in the east and shone brightly. Both were soon out on the dyke again and looking across towards Jevershallig which lay like a patch of mist over the water. "It's moving about again," said the farmhand; "I was here just after mid-day: it wasn't there then, but I clearly saw the horse's skeleton lying there!"

The boy craned his neck. "But it's not there now, Iven," he whispered.

"Well, Carsten, what about it?" said the farmhand. "Still itching to row out there?"

Carsten reflected for a moment; then he cracked his whip in the air. "Cast off the boat, Iven!" he said.

Across the water whatever it was that was moving over there

seemed to raise its head and look towards the mainland. They saw it no longer; they had already gone down the side of the dyke to the spot where the boat was moored. "Well, climb in!" said the farmhand after he had loosened the rope. "I'll stay here till you come back! You need to beach on the eastern side; it's always been possible to land there!" And the boy silently nodded and rowed out into the moonlit night with his whip; the farmhand ambled back along the bottom of the dyke and clambered back up to where they had been standing. He soon saw the boat being moored across the water near a steep dark spot, towards which a wide watercourse ran, and a stocky figure scramble out onto the shore. – Wasn't the boy cracking his whip? But it might well be the noise from the incoming tide. He saw, several hundred paces northwards, what they had taken to be a horse; and now! – yes, the figure of the boy was walking directly towards it. It lifted its head, as if startled by something; and the boy – as could now clearly be heard – cracked his whip. But – what was he thinking of? He turned round, going back the way he had come. The thing over there seemed to go on grazing, not a whinny had been heard; it appeared occasionally as if ribbons of white foam were being drawn over the apparition. The farmhand looked spellbound across at the hallig.

Then he heard the boat being beached on the near shore and soon saw through the twilight the figure of the boy clambering up the side of the dyke towards him. "Well, Carsten," he asked, "what was it?"

The boy shook his head. "It was nothing!" he said. "I saw it a little while from the boat; but then, when I was on the hallig – I'm hanged if I know where that animal disappeared to, the moon was definitely bright enough, but when I reached the spot there was nothing there but the bleached bones of half a dozen sheep, and a bit further on the horse's skeleton with its long white skull and the moon shining into its empty eye-sockets!"

"Oh!" said the farmhand. "Did you take a really good look at it!"

"Of course, Iven, I was standing right beside it. Then a god-forsaken lapwing, which had hidden itself away behind the skeleton to sleep, suddenly flew up screeching and so startled me that I cracked my whip a couple of times after it."

"And that was all?"

"Yes, Iven; that's all I know."

"It's quite enough," said the farmhand, pulling the boy by the arm towards him and pointing towards the hallig. "There, see anything, Carsten?"

"You're right, it's there again!"

"Again?" said the farmhand. "I've been looking over there the whole time, but not once did it move; you walked straight up to the evil thing!"

The boy stared at him; a look of horror suddenly spread across his normally cheeky face, and even the farmhand did not fail to notice it. "Come on!" he said, "let's be off home: it looks alive from here, and there're just bones lying over there – it's beyond the likes of us! But keep quiet about this, things like this should-n't be talked about!"

They turned away, and the boy hurried along by his side; they did not speak, and the marsh lay quiet and still beside them.

After the moon had waned and the nights had grown dark, something else happened.

Hauke Haien had ridden to the town on the day of the horse market without, however, having any business to transact. Nevertheless, coming home towards evening, he brought a second horse home with him; but it was coarse-haired and so thin that every one of its ribs could be counted, and the eyes lay dull and sunken in their sockets. Elke had come to the door to welcome her husband home: "Heaven help us!" she cried. "What do we want with that old grey?" For as Hauke came riding up to the front of the house with it and stopped under the ash tree, she noticed that the poor creature was lame too.

But the young dykemaster jumped down laughing from his chestnut gelding. "Don't worry, Elke, it didn't cost much!"

"You know very well," answered his prudent wife, "that the cheapest can often be the most expensive in the end."

"But not always, Elke. The animal's four years old at the most, look closely at him! He's been starved and ill-treated; our oats will do him good; I'll look after him myself to make sure he's not over-fed."

The animal, meanwhile, stood with head drooped, long mane

70

hanging down about its neck. While her husband called the farmhands, Frau Elke walked round the horse looking at it; but she shook her head. "We've never had a horse like this in our stable before!"

When the servant boy came round the corner of the house, he stopped suddenly with a frightened look in his eyes. "Well, Carsten," cried the dykemaster, "what's got into you? Don't you like my new grey?"

"Yes – of course, Squire. Why not?"

"Then put the horses in the stable; don't feed them; I'll be there myself in a minute!"

The boy cautiously took hold of the grey's halter, then at the same time, as though for protection, hastily grabbed the reins of the gelding which had also been entrusted to him. Hauke went with his wife into the living room; she had prepared some mulled ale for him, and bread and butter too was laid out on the table.

He had soon eaten his fill; then rising from the table he walked up and down the room with his wife. "Let me explain, Elke," he said, as the evening light played on the tiles on the walls, "just how I came by the animal. I suppose I'd been with the chief dykemaster for an hour; he had excellent news for me – there may be one change or another to my outline drawings, but the main thing, the shape of the dyke, has been accepted, and within the next few days the order for the building of the new dyke might come!"

Elke gave an involuntary sigh. "Then what?" she asked anxiously.

"Well, Elke," replied Hauke, "there'll be a lot of hard work, but I think the good Lord brought us together for this! Our farm is in good order; you can now shoulder a good deal of the work yourself; just think ten years ahead – our property will be quite a different one."

His first words had made her clasp her husband's hand securely within hers but his last words had upset her. "Who will this property be for?" she said. "You'll have to get yourself another wife; I'm not going to give you any children."

Tears started in her eyes; but he took her firmly in his arms. "We'll leave that to God," he said. "We're young enough now, and will still be in the future, to enjoy the fruits of our labours ourselves."

71

For a long while she looked at him with her dark eyes as he held her. "I'm sorry, Hauke," she said; "I'm a faint-hearted wife at times!"

He bent down and kissed her. "You're my wife and I'm your husband, Elke! And it will never be otherwise."

She put her arms tightly round his neck. "You're right, Hauke, and whatever happens, happens to us both." Then, blushing, she released herself from him. "You wanted to tell me about the grey," she said softly.

"Yes, I did, Elke, As I was saying, my head was in a whirl at the good news the chief dykemaster had given me, and I was just riding out of the town again when, on the Damm behind the harbour, I met a scruffy-looking fellow; I couldn't make out if he was a vagabond, a tinker or what. The fellow was leading the grey by its halter, and the animal raised its head and looked at me with dull eyes; I had the feeling it wanted to ask me for something; and I was rich enough at that moment. 'Heh, countryman!' I shouted, 'where are you going with that old nag?'

"The fellow stopped, so did the grey. 'To sell it!' he said, and nodded slyly in my direction.

"'Not to me you won't!' I said with a laugh.

"'I certainly will!' he said; 'that's a stout horse, and worth every bit of a hundred thaler.'

"I laughed in his face.

"'Well,' he said, 'I shouldn't laugh so hard, I'm not asking you to pay all that for it! I've got no use for it; with me it's being neglected; it would soon look different with you!'

"Then I jumped down from my gelding and looked in the horse's mouth, and I saw that it was still a young animal. 'What do you want for it then?' I asked, as the horse again looked at me pleadingly.

"'Sir, take it for thirty thaler!' said the fellow, 'and I'll throw the halter in for good measure!'

"And then, Elke, I shook the fellow's offered brown hand on it, which looked almost like a claw. So we have the grey, at a very good price I believe! But it was all so strange; as I rode away with the horses, right behind me I heard a laugh, and when I turned my head I saw the Slovak standing with his legs wide apart, hands on his hips, and he was laughing like a devil at me behind my back."

"Oh dear!" cried Elke. "Let's hope he hasn't brought any of his old master's ways with him and fares better here with you, Hauke!"

"He'll at least do that, if I have anything to do with it!" And the dykemaster went into the stable as he had earlier told the boy he would do.

Not only on that evening but from then on he fed the grey himself and never let it out of his sight; he wanted to show that he had struck a good bargain; at least nothing would be overlooked. – And after only a few weeks the condition of the animal improved; the coarse hair gradually disappeared; a shiny, bluish-grey speckled coat began to appear, and when he led it around the courtyard one day, it walked smoothly on firm legs. Hauke's thoughts were of the wild-looking horse-dealer. "The fellow was either a fool or a rogue – who had stolen it!" he murmured to himself. Before long the horse in the stable only had to hear his footsteps and it would swiftly turn its head and whinny in his direction; he also noticed it had what an Arab horse should have: a thin fleshless face, from which blazed two fiery brown eyes. He led it out of the stable and strapped a light saddle onto its back. He was hardly mounted when it let out a whinny like a cry of pleasure from its throat, and flew off with him down the side of the earthwork onto the road, then on towards the dyke; but the rider sat firmly in the saddle, and when they were on top of the dyke it calmed to a light, almost prancing gait and turned its head towards the sea. He patted and caressed its shiny neck, but it was no longer in need of this caress; the horse appeared to be completely at one with its rider, and after they had ridden a stretch northwards along the top of the dyke, he turned it round easily and rode back to the farmstead.

The farmhands stood at the foot of the earthwork waiting for their employer's return. "Right then, Iven," said Hauke, springing down from his horse, "now you can ride him out to the others in the fen; he'll carry you like a baby in a cradle!"

The grey shook its head and whinnied loud across the sunlit marshscape while the farmhand unbuckled the saddle and the boy ran with it to the tack-room; then it laid its head on its master's shoulder and submitted quietly to his caress. But when the farmhand tried to swing himself up onto its back, the horse started suddenly to one side and stood motionless again, its beautiful eyes focused on its master. "Did he hurt you, Iven?" cried Hauke, and he attempted to help the boy up from the ground.

The lad vigorously rubbed his hip. "No, sir, I'm all right; but let the devil ride that grey!"

"And me!" added Hauke, with a laugh. "Then take him out to the fen on the rein!"

And when the farmhand, somewhat ashamed, obeyed, the grey let itself be quietly led away.

A few evenings later the farmhand and the stable boy stood together by the stable door; behind the dyke the sunset had died away and inside the dyke the polder was already sunk in deep twilight; only once in a while from a distance came the lowing of a startled cow or the shriek of a lark whose life had been ended by an attack from a weasel or a water-rat. The farmhand was leaning against the stable doorpost smoking a short pipe, whose smoke he could no longer see; he and the boy had not yet spoken to each other. The latter, however, had something weighing on his mind, only he did not know how to broach the subject with the silent farmhand. "Heh, Iven!" he said finally, "you know that horse's skeleton on Jeverssand?"

"What about it?" asked the farmhand.

"Yes, Iven, what about it? It's simply not there anymore, that's all; not by daylight and not by moonlight; a good twenty times I've been up onto that dyke!"

"I suppose the old bones must have simply collapsed in a heap," said Iven, continuing to smoke.

"But I was out there in the moonlight, and there was nothing on Jeverssand!"

"Of course not," said Iven, "it's simply fallen apart so it can't stand up anymore, that's all!"

"Don't joke about it, Iven! Now I know; I can tell you where it is!"

Iven turned suddenly towards him. "Well, where is it then?"

"Where is it?" repeated the boy, emphasising the words. "It's standing in our stable; it's been standing there since it's no longer been on the hallig! The dykemaster doesn't feed it himself for no reason. I know what I'm talking about, Iven!"

74

The farmhand puffed heavily on his pipe for a while into the night air. "You're not being very quick-witted, Carsten," he then said. "Our grey? If ever a horse was alive, that one surely is! How can a sharp lad like you be swayed by old wives' tales?"

But the boy would not be put off: if the devil were inside the grey, why shouldn't it be lively? Just the opposite, it would make it so much the worse! He started in terror every time he entered the stable in which the animal was occasionally kept for the night, even in the summer, and it suddenly swung its fiery head round to face him. "The devil take it!" he would growl, "We shan't be together for very much longer, I can tell you!"

So he began secretly to look around for other work, gave in his notice, and around All Saints' Day entered into employment with Ole Peters as a farmhand. Here he found reverent listeners for his story of the dykemaster's satanic horse; the buxom Frau Vollina and her senile father, the former dyke commissioner Jess Harders, listened in delighted horror and afterwards told it to everyone who bore a grudge in their hearts against the dykemaster, or who simply loved to hear about such things.

✳ ✳

The order from the chief dykemaster's office to dyke the foreland had arrived by the end of March. Hauke first called the dyke commissioners together, and they gathered up at the inn beside the church to listen as he read them the main points from the prepared documents: from his proposal, from the chief dykemaster's report, and lastly the final decision, which above all included the acceptance of his proposed new shape for the dyke – not steep on its seaward side as before but with a gradual slope; they listened, however, with neither pleased nor even satisfied expressions on their faces.

"So," said an old commissioner; "now we have the reckoning, and it will be no good protesting since our dykemaster here is obviously backed by the chief dykemaster!"

"You're right, Detlev Wiens," added a second; "the spring work's upon us, and now miles of dyke are supposed to be built as well – everything will have to be left."

"But it can still be finished this year," said Hauke; "the new dyke can't be built in a day!"

There were few who would accept this. "But your shape!" said a third, finding a new objection; "the dyke on the seaward side will be so wide it will make the Lawrence Boy look like a midget! Where's all the material going to come from? When is the work supposed to be finished?"

"If not this year, then next; it'll be largely up to us!" said Hauke.

Angry laughter swept through the assembled company. "But why all the useless work? The dyke's not going to be any higher than the old one," shouted a new voice; "and I reckon that's been standing there for well over thirty years now!"

"What you say is quite right," said Hauke. "Thirty years ago the old dyke was breached, and thirty-five years before that, and forty-five years before that; but since then, even though it's been standing there, steep and against all reason, the highest tides have spared us. But the new dyke, whatever the weather, will stand for hundreds and hundreds of years; it will never be breached because the gentle slope on its seaward side will not give the waves any direct point of impact, and so you'll be gaining a safe polder for yourselves and for your children – that's why the authorities and the chief dykemaster have backed my scheme, and why you ought to realise it's for your own good!"

When the gathering did not immediately respond, a white-haired old man struggled up out of his chair; it was Frau Elke's godfather, Jewe Manners, who had remained in his post as dyke commissioner at Hauke's request. "Dykemaster Hauke Haien," he said, "you put us to a lot of trouble and cost, and I would have preferred it if you had waited until the good Lord had laid me to rest; but – you are right, and a man would have to be stupid to deny it. As every day passes we have God to thank for preserving that precious stretch of foreland against storm and flood for us, in spite of our indolence; but now is the eleventh hour when we ourselves must lend a hand to safeguard it, use all our knowledge and ability in doing so, and stop trying God's patience any further. I, my friends, am an old man; I have seen dykes built and breached; but the dyke which Hauke Haien has planned through God-given insight, and for which he has gained approval from the authorities, not one of you will ever see breached in your lifetime, and if you won't thank him yourselves, then your grandchildren certainly won't be able to deny him the laurel crown one day!"

Jewe Manners sat down again, took his blue handkerchief from his pocket and wiped a few beads of sweat from his brow. The old man was still recognised to be a highly competent and scrupulously honest man, and since the gathering was simply not inclined to agree with him, it remained silent. Hauke Haien took the floor; everyone saw that his face had paled. "Thank you, Jewe Manners," he said, "for still being here and for the words you have spoken. I hope you other dyke commissioners will see the new dyke, whose workload will certainly fall on me, at least as something that cannot be put off. Let us decide, therefore, what needs to be done!"

"Tell us!" said one of the dyke commissioners. And Hauke spread the plan of the new dyke out on the table. "Someone asked earlier," he began, "where so much earth is to come from? – You see, all along here where the foreland projects into the tidal flats, a strip of land outside the line of the dyke has been left free; we can take the earth from there and from the foreland that runs northwards and southwards from the new polder beside the old dyke; if we have a solid layer of clay on the seaward side, on the landward side or in the middle we can mostly use sand! – But first a surveyor needs to be appointed who will peg out the line of the new dyke across the foreland. The one who helped me prepare the plan will be the best suited for the task, I imagine. And for transporting clay and the like we shall need to contract wainwrights to make us some horse-drawn tip-carts with shafts; I can't say yet how many hundreds of cart-loads of straw we shall need for laying, pinning and fixing to the dyke, for the damming of the watercourse and for the landward side of the dyke – where perhaps we shall have to be satisfied with sand – and perhaps a lot more than will be available here in the marsh! So let's first of all discuss how we're going to obtain and organise all this material; later we'll need a capable carpenter to build the new sluice here on the west side fronting the sea."

Those present at the meeting had gathered round the table, half-eyeing the plan, and gradually began to speak; but they seemed to be doing so only for the sake of saying something. On the matter of choosing a surveyor, one of the younger ones said: "You've worked it all out, dykemaster; you must know best who's the right man for the job."

But Hauke retorted: "Since you're members of the dyke committee, you must voice your own opinions, not mine, Jakob Meyen; and if you've got a better proposal, I'll withdraw mine!"

"No, yours will be all right," said Jakob Meyen.

But for one of the older commissioners it was not all right; he had a nephew, a surveyor, with skills never seen before here in the marsh; he was said to be even better than the dykemaster's father, the late Tede Haien!

So both surveyors were discussed and it was finally agreed that they should undertake the work jointly. The same pattern was followed for the tip-carts, as was the supply of straw and everything else, and Hauke arrived home on the gelding he still rode at that time, at a late hour and almost completely exhausted. But scarcely had he sat down in the old armchair that had belonged to his weighty and less active predecessor, when his wife was there by his side. "You look so tired, Hauke," she said, and gently brushed his hair away from his brow with her slim hand.

"A little!" he replied.

"Was everything all right?"

"You could say so," he said with a bitter smile, "but I'm going to have to get the wheels turning myself and be glad when they aren't stopped!"

"Surely not by everyone?"

"No, Elke; your godfather, Jewe Manners, is a good man; but I wish he were thirty years younger."

✢ ✢

When after some weeks the line of the dyke had been pegged out and most of the tip-carts had been supplied, the dykemaster called all the owners of shares in the land to be dyked, together with the owners of the fields situated behind the old dyke, to a meeting in the village inn, to present a plan for the allocation of work and costs and to hear objections if there were any; for the owners of the fields behind the old dyke were also to be asked to do their share of the work and to bear their share of the cost in

78

so far as the new dyke and sluices would reduce the maintenance costs of the old one. This matter had been a difficult one for Hauke to carry through, and if he had not been allocated a dyke messenger as well as a dyke clerk by the chief dykemaster, he would not have been able to finish the work so soon, even though each day's work had again continued well into the night. And when at last, dead tired, he sought his bed, Elke would not be waiting up for him in feigned sleep as before; she too had her full measure of daily work and lay asleep at night as though she were at the bottom of a deep well.

When Hauke had read out his scheme and spread out his papers on the table again – papers that had been available for the last three days for everyone to see in the inn – there were serious-minded men present who viewed this conscientious industry with respect, and after calm reflection accepted the dykemaster's fair estimates; but others, whose interests in the new land had been sold off either by themselves or by their fathers or by other former owners, complained that they were being dragged against their will into meeting the costs of the new polder, land which was no longer any of their concern, preferring to forget that as a result of the new work their old land too by and by would be less burdened by demands for labour or contributions to costs; and there were yet others who, possessed of shares in the new polder, shouted loudly that anyone was welcome to them at any price, for the unfair burden they would bring could not be tolerated. Ole Peters, however, who leaned against the doorpost with a grim expression on his face, interrupted: "Think about it first, then trust our dyke-master! He can do his sums, he can; he already had the majority of shares, and knew how to persuade me to part with mine. And when he had them too, he decided to dyke this new polder!"

After these words were spoken there was a moment of deathly silence in the gathering. The dykemaster stood at the table on which he had earlier spread out his papers and, lifting his head, looked across at Ole Peters. "You know only too well, Ole Peters," he said, "that you slander me; but you do so because you know that a fair bit of the mud you throw at me will stick! The truth is that you wanted to get rid of your shares and I needed them at the time for my sheep-breeding; and if you must know, that cheap remark you made in this inn about me being dykemaster simply because of my wife – that provoked me, and I wanted to show you that I could be dykemaster on my own account; and therefore, Ole Peters, I did what the dykemaster before me should have done. If you have a grudge against me because your shares became mine at that time – you have just heard that there are plenty of people around offering their shares cheaply because the work is too much for them!"

From a small part of the gathering came murmured approval, and old Jewe Manners who was standing there cried out: "Bravo, Hauke Haien! Our Lord will make you succeed in your work!"

But they did not complete all the business, even though Ole Peters kept silent and the meeting continued until everyone went home for supper; only at a second meeting was everything settled, but only after Hauke had promised four teams of wagons and horses for the following month instead of the three he was obliged to provide.

Finally, when the Whitsun bells were ringing out across the land, the work had begun: the tip-carts ceaselessly journeyed from the foreland to the line of the dyke to deliver the clay, and the same number were already returning to the foreland to be loaded up again; on the line of the dyke itself stood men with shovels and spades moving the cartloads of clay to the right place and levelling it off; enormous loads of straw were driven up and unloaded, not only as cover for lighter materials such as sand and loose soil which were used on the landward sides, but also, as stretches of the sea-facing slopes were gradually completed, as a secure matting over the turfs that had been laid to protect the slopes from the gnawing waves. Appointed foremen walked up and down, and when it blew a gale they stood with wide-open mouths hollering their orders into the wind and weather; among them rode the dykemaster on his grey, which he now used all the time, and the animal flew to and fro with its rider as he swiftly and coldly rapped out his orders, praised the workmen, or, as happened from time to time, dismissed a lazy or clumsy worker without mercy. "That's no use!" he would shout; "we can't allow your idleness to ruin this dyke!" When he rode up from the polder the snorting of his horse could be heard from afar, and every hand set to work more swiftly. "Look sharp there! The dykemaster's coming!"

Around breakfast-time, when the workmen sat on the ground in groups with their food, Hauke would ride along the abandoned line of work, his keen eyes sharp to spot where the spades had been wielded by slipshod hands. But when he rode up to the workmen and explained to them how the work had to be done, they simply looked up at him and carried on patiently chewing their bread; he never heard a word of agreement or even a comment from them. Once at such at time, though it was getting late, when he had found the work at one place on the dyke in an especially satisfactory state, he rode up to the nearest group of men having their breakfast, sprang down from his grey and asked cheerily who had done such good work; but the men just looked at him with sullen mistrust, and only gradually were a few names reluctantly mentioned. The man to whom he had given his horse, which was standing quiet as a lamb, held it with both hands and looked anxiously at the animal's beautiful eyes which as usual remained fixed on its master.

"What is it, Marten?" called Hauke. "You look as though you've been struck by lightning!"

"Sir, your horse, it's so still; as though it's up to no good!"

Hauke laughed and took the horse by the reins himself; it at once rubbed its head affectionately against his shoulder. A few of the workmen looked warily across at the horse and rider, but others, as if none of it were any concern of theirs, ate in silence, now and then throwing a piece of bread up to the seagulls which, having espied where there was food, beating their slender wings almost settled on the mens' heads. The dykemaster gazed blankly for a while at the scavenging birds and watched as they caught the thrown-up scraps in their bills; then he sprang up into the saddle and rode off without looking back at the men; some words now spoken aloud among them sounded to him close to ridicule. "What is it?" he said to himself. "Was Elke right after all – that they are all against me? Even these farmhands and small folk, so many of whom will prosper because of my new dyke?"

He dug his spurs into his horse so that it flew wildly down onto the polder. He knew nothing of the sinister light in which the rider on the grey had been painted by his former stable lad; but if only they could have seen him now, his eyes staring from his gaunt face, his cloak flying in the wind, the grey glinting and flashing!

81

Summer and autumn passed; the work went steadily on until the end of November when the frost and snow brought it to an end; and since it was unfinished it was decided to leave the polder open to the sea. The dyke now rose nearly eight feet above the level of the polder, and only in the westward section fronting the sea where the sluice was going to be installed had a gap been left in it; in the northern part too, in front of the old dyke, the watercourse was still untouched. The tide, therefore, as it had done over the last thirty years, could run into the polder without doing extensive damage to it or to the new dyke. And so the creation of man was entrusted to God and placed under His protection until the spring sun could make its completion possible.

Preparations meanwhile had been made in the dykemaster's house for a joyous occasion: in the ninth year of the marriage a child had been born. It was red and wrinkled and weighed the seven pounds expected of newly-born children if, as this one did, they belong to the female sex; but its cries were strangely muffled, which the midwife had not liked at all. Worst of all, however, on the third day Elke was struck down with childbed fever, became delirious and recognised neither her husband nor her old maid. The unrestrained joy that had gripped Hauke at the sight of his child had turned into sorrow. The doctor was fetched from the town; he sat on the bed, felt her pulse, prescribed some medicine, but was at a complete loss. Hauke shook his head. "He can't help; only God can help!" He had worked out his own version of Christianity, but there was something that restrained his prayer. When the old doctor had ridden off he stood by the window staring out at the wintry day, and while the sick woman cried out in delirium, clasped his hands together, whether to pray or simply to prevent himself from sinking into immense fear he did not himself know.

"Water! The water!" the sick woman whimpered. "Hold me!" she cried; "hold me, Hauke!" Then her voice faded; it sounded as though she were sobbing. "Out to sea, into the shallows? O dear God, I'll never see him again!"

Hauke turned and pushed the midwife away from the bed; he fell on his knees, put his arms round his wife and pulled her to him. "Elke! Elke, look at me, I'm here!"

But she just opened wide her feverish eyes and gazed around as though beyond all hope of rescue.

He laid her back onto her pillows, then folded his hands together. "Lord, my God," he cried, "don't take her from me! You know I can't do without her!" Then, as though reflecting, he added quietly: "I know that You cannot always do what You wish, not even You; You are omniscient; You must do according to Your wisdom – but O Lord, speak to me in just a whisper!"

It was as if a stillness had suddenly descended; he heard only a quiet breathing; when he turned towards the bed his wife lay in a peaceful sleep, but the midwife was looking at him with horrified eyes. He heard the door close. "Who was that?" he asked.

"The maid, Sir: Ann Grete has gone out; she'd brought the warming pan."

"Why are you looking so frightened, Frau Levke?"

"Me? Your prayer shocked me; you'll never save a soul from death with a prayer like that, no never!"

Hauke looked at her with his piercing eyes. "Do you too, like our Ann Grete, go to the conventicle meetings held by that Dutch tailor, Jantje?"

"Yes; we both have the living faith!"

Hauke did not answer her. The separatist conventicle movement had rapidly become popular at that time and had blossomed among the Friesians; ruined artisans and schoolmasters sacked for drunkenness played leading roles in it, and loose girls, young and old women, idlers and friendless people, eagerly attended the secret meetings in which any one of them could play the part of priest. Of the dykemaster's household, Ann Grete and the stable boy she loved would spend their free evenings there. Elke had certainly not kept her reservations about it from Hauke; but it was his opinion that in matters of belief no one should seek to influence another: it did no harm, and better to be there than at the inn!

So that was how it had been left, and on this occasion too he said nothing more about it. Nobody, however, kept quiet about him; the words of his prayer were passed around from house to house: he had questioned God's omnipotence, but what was a God without omnipotence? He was an atheist; the business about the devil's horse might well be true after all!

Hauke learned nothing of this; he had eyes and ears only for his wife, and even the child no longer existed for him.

The old doctor came again, he came every day, occasionally twice, then stayed a whole night, wrote another prescription, and the farmhand, Iven Johns, rode hard with it to the pharmacy. Then his face brightened and he nodded confidentially to the dykemaster: "It's going to be all right! It's going to be all right! With God's help!" And one day – had his medical skills overcome the illness, or had God, through Hauke's prayer, been able to find a way after all? – when the doctor was alone with the sick woman, he spoke to her, and his old eyes sparkled. "Frau, I can now truly say to you that today is the doctor's day of celebration; your condition was serious, but now you belong to us again, to the living!"

Her dark eyes were pools of radiance. "Hauke! Hauke, where are you?" she cried, and when at her clear call he rushed into her room and to her bedside, she flung her arms round his neck. "Hauke, my husband, saved! I am with you still!"

The old doctor drew his silk handkerchief from his pocket, wiped it over his brow and cheeks, then left the room with many a nod.

Three evenings later a pious preacher – a slipper-maker previously dismissed from his work by the dykemaster – spoke at one of the Dutch tailor's conventicle meetings and was explaining the nature of God to his listeners: "Whoever denies the omnipotence of God, whoever says: 'I know You cannot do as You wish' – we all know this unrepentant sinner; he's like a stone round the community's neck – he has fallen from God and seeks the enemy of God, the friend of sin, as his comforter; for man's hand must reach out for some kind of staff. But beware the man who prays in this way, for his prayer is a curse!"

This too circulated from house to house. What is not passed on in a small community? And it also reached Hauke's ears. He spoke no word about it, even to his wife; but occasionally he would pull her towards him and hold her tightly in his arms. "Stay true to me, Elke! Stay true!" She looked at him, her eyes full of bewilderment. "True to you? Who else should I be true

84

to?" But after a brief moment she understood the meaning of his words. "Yes, Hauke, we're true to each other; not only because we need each other." Then they both went off to attend to their work.

By and large all would have been well, but in spite of the intense activity, a loneliness surrounded him, and in his heart an attitude of defiance and isolation towards other people was sown; only towards his wife did he remain the same, and in the mornings and evenings he would kneel down before his child's cradle as though that were the place where he would find his eternal salvation. Towards servants and workmen, however, he became more severe; the incompetent and the negligent, whom previously he had set right with a mild scolding, were now startled by his harsh outbursts, and from time to time Elke went quietly among them to repair the damage.

※ ※

Work on the dyke resumed as spring approached; a temporary dyke, half-moon-shaped on both its seaward and landward sides, was built to close the gap in the western section of the dyke and to protect the new sluice that now had to be built; and as the sluice grew steadily in height, so the new dyke grew even more rapidly to its final height. The dykemaster's work did not get easier, for in place of Jewe Manners who had died during the winter, Ole Peters had been appointed a dyke commissioner. Hauke had not sought to prevent it, but instead of the encouraging words and the warm-hearted pats on his left shoulder that he had so often received from his wife's old godfather, he now received from his successor only concealed resistance and unnecessary objections which had to be met with equally unnecessary explanations; for although Ole was one of those who carried some weight, in dyke matters he was not one of those with intelligence; the 'scribbling' farmhand of former times still stood in his way.

A most radiant sky spread itself once more over the sea and the marsh, and again the polder was brought to colourful life by the sturdy cattle whose lowing occasionally broke the widespread silence; high in the sky the larks sang ceaselessly, but were noticed only when, for the length of a breath, their song fell silent. The work was not interrupted by bad weather and the sluice was already standing with its unpainted timbers without ever having needed, even for a night, the protection of the temporary dyke; God appeared to look favourably on the new creation. Frau Elke's eyes too were full of joy for her husband when he came home from the dyke on his grey. "You've turned into a fine animal after all!" she said to the horse, patting its glistening neck. But if she was holding the child, Hauke would spring down from his horse and bob the tiny tot up and down in his arms, and if the horse kept its brown eyes fixed on the child, Hauke would say: "Come on then; you can have the honour too!" And he would lift little Wienke – for that is what she had been christened – up into the saddle and lead the horse in a circle round the top of the earthwork. Even the old ash tree occasionally had the honour, for he would sit the child on a swaying branch and rock her up and down. The mother stood in the doorway with laughter in her eyes; but the child did not laugh, her eyes, between which a fine little nose was set, gazed somewhat impassively into the distance and the small hands made no attempt to grasp the short stick her father held out towards her. Hauke failed to notice it, he knew nothing about such small children; only Elke, when she saw the bright-eyed girl in the arms of her housemaid who had had her baby at the same time, would sometimes remark anxiously: "My child's not as advanced as yours, Stina!" and the woman, lovingly shaking her plump little boy, whom she held by the hand, would reply: "Well, ma'am, children are all different – this one here was stealing apples out of the larder when he was still two!" Elke brushed the plump little lad's curly hair away from his eyes and then, without being noticed, pressed her quiet child to her heart.

By the beginning of October the new sluice stood solidly on the western side between the two converging sections of the new sea dyke. The dyke's gentle slope on the seaward side extended all the way round except for the gaps left for the watercourse; it rose about fifteen feet above normal tide-level, and from its north-west corner there was an uninterrupted view past Jevershallig to the North Sea tidal flats; the winds here, however, had a much sharper bite to them; one's hair flew in the wind, and anyone wanting to watch from here needed to have his cap firmly set on his head.

By the end of November, when the storms and the rains began, it only remained to fill the gap close to the old dyke through which the sea rushed into the new polder along the bed of the water-course on the north side. On both sides of the gap stood the steep walls of the dyke; the void between them had now to be filled. The work would have been much easier in dry summer weather, but it had to be done even under the present conditions, for a sudden storm could endanger the whole undertaking. And Hauke now staked everything on getting the job finished. The rain poured down, the wind whistled; but his lean figure astride the fiery grey would emerge, now here, now there, from out of the dark masses of workmen who were toiling at the top and bottom of the dyke on its northern side by the gap. Now he could be seen down by the tip-carts that had transported the clay all the way from the fore-land and were just arriving in a jostling mass by the deep water-course to tip out their loads there. The dykemaster's brisk words of command rang out from time to time through the splatter of the rain and the roar of the wind; he wanted to be in sole charge here today; he called each cart up in turn and ordered back those which were impatiently pushing their way forward. "Stop!" he called out, and the work below paused. "Straw! A load of straw down here!" he shouted up to the men on top, and from one of the waiting carts above a load of hay fell down onto the wet clay below. There men sprang amongst it, ripping it apart, and shouting to the men above not to bury them with any more. More new carts arrived, and Hauke was once again up on the dyke looking down from his grey into the gap and watching the shovelling and tipping that was going on; then he turned his gaze out to sea. It was blowing hard and he saw the line of foaming surf clawing its way further and further up the side of the dyke and the waves rid-ing even higher; he also saw the men dripping with water and scarcely able to breathe in their strenuous work because of the wind which snatched their breath away and the cold rain which streamed down on them. "Keep at it, men! Keep at it!" he shout-ed down to them. "Only a foot or two higher, then it's enough for this tide!" And through all the din of the storm the noise of the workmen could be heard: the splatter of the tipped clay, the rattle of the carts, the rustle of the straw as it was dropped down, all went on without a pause. Through the noise, from time to time, could be heard the whimper of a little golden-haired dog which, frozen and as if lost, was being driven here and there among the men and the carts; suddenly the small animal's pitiful cry rang out from below in the gap. Hauke looked down; he had caught sight of it being hurled from above; a sudden flush of anger rose in his face. "Stop! Stop it!" he shouted to the carts below; for the tipping of the wet clay continued without pause.

"What for?" a rough voice shouted up from below. "Surely not for that miserable cur?"

"Stop it, I say!" shouted Hauke again. "Fetch the dog to me! I won't have any such crime on this dyke!"

But not a hand moved, only a few more spadefuls of thick clay flew next to the squealing animal. He dug his spurs into the grey so that it neighed loudly and plunged down the side of the dyke, and everyone shrank back before him. "The dog!" he cried; "I want the dog!"

A hand gently tapped his shoulder as if it were the hand of old Jewe Manners; but when he looked round it was only a friend of the old man. "Be careful, dykemaster!" he whispered. "You've no friends among these men; let the dog be!"

The wind whistled, the rain lashed down; the men had stuck their spades into the ground, some had thrown them away. Hauke bent towards the old man. "Hold my grey for me, will you, Harke Jens?" he asked, but the man had hardly taken hold of the reins before Hauke had jumped down into the gap and was holding the small whimpering animal in his arms, and almost in the same instant he was again astride the saddle and springing back up the dyke. His eyes darted over the men who stood by the carts. "Who was it?" he demanded. "Who threw this animal down there?"

For a moment no one spoke, the dykemaster's gaunt face flared with anger, and they were gripped by a superstitious fear of him. Then from one of the carts a bull-necked fellow strode up in front of him. "It wasn't me, dykemaster," he said, biting the end off a small piece of chewing tobacco and putting it calmly into his mouth; "but whoever did it, did right; if your dyke's going to hold, something live's got to go into it!"

"Something live? What catechism did you learn that from?"

"None, sir!" replied the fellow with an impudent laugh; "even our grandfathers knew that and they were every bit as good Christians as you are! A child's best of all; but when there's none to be had, a dog will do!"

"Stop your pagan teachings!" shouted Hauke at him. "It would fill the hole better if we threw you into it."

"Oho!" rang the response; the sound came from a dozen throats, and the dykemaster became aware of enraged faces and clenched fists around him; he saw clearly that there was not a friend among them. The thought of his dyke struck him with sudden terror: what would happen if they should all now throw their spades away? – But when he looked below, he saw old Jewe Manners' friend again; he was walking among the men, speaking to this or that person, giving one a friendly laugh, patting another on the shoulder with an amicable smile, and one after the other they gripped their spades again; a few moments later the work was again in full progress. – What more did he want? The watercourse had to be closed off, and he kept the dog safely hidden away within the folds of his coat. With sudden resolve he turned his grey towards the next cart. "Straw up to the edge!" he firmly commanded, and mechanically the driver obeyed him; it soon fell swishing downwards into the depths below and on all sides work began again with renewed vigour.

The work had continued for a further hour; it was gone six o'clock and a deep twilight was already falling; it had stopped raining. Hauke called the foremen to his horse. "Tomorrow morning at four o'clock," he said; "everyone's to be here; the moon will still be up; and with God's help we'll finish it! And one more thing!" he shouted when they were about to leave. "Do you know this dog?" And he took the trembling animal out of his coat.

No-one said he did; but someone said: "It's been scavenging around the village for days; it doesn't belong to a soul!"

"Then he's mine!" retorted Hauke. "Don't forget: tomorrow morning at four o'clock!" And he rode off.

When he arrived home, Ann Grete was just coming out of the door; her clothes were neat and clean and it suddenly occurred to him that she might be on her way to the conventicle tailor. "Hold your apron out!" he called down to her, and as she instinctively obeyed, he threw the small, clay-bespattered dog into it. "Take him along to little Wienke; he's to be a playmate for her! But wash and warm him up first; you'll be doing God's good work too, for the animal's frozen stiff."

Ann Grete could not afford to disobey her employer, so did not go to the conventicle that evening.

✻ ✻

On the following day the last spade-thrust was made on the new dyke; the wind had calmed; seagulls and avocets glided to and fro in graceful flight over the land and water; from Jevershallig came the sound of a thousand-voiced chorus of honking brent geese which were still content to linger on the North Sea coast, and out of the grey early morning mists which blanketed the broad marshland there gradually emerged a golden autumn day which shed its light upon this new work of men's hands.

Some weeks later the Royal Government Commissioners came with the chief dykemaster to inspect the new dyke. A great banquet, the first since old Tede Volkerts' funeral, was held in the dykemaster's house, and all the dyke commissioners and the biggest landowners were invited. After the meal the dykemaster's and guests' carriages were hitched to their horses. The chief dykemaster lifted Frau Elke up into the trap in front of which stood the brown gelding stamping its hoofs, then sprang up next to her and took the reins into his hands; he wanted to drive his dykemaster's clever wife himself. And so the party set out gaily from the earthwork and along the track up to the new dyke, then along it round the new polder. A light north-west wind had sprung up in the meantime and on the north and west sides of the new dyke the tide rose; nobody could fail to see that the gentle slope caused less wave impact; such high praise for the dykemaster poured from the mouths of the Royal Government Commissioners that the local dyke commissioners' intermittently voiced reservations were soon stifled entirely.

This too passed; but the dykemaster gained further satisfaction as he rode along the top of the dyke one day quietly absorbed in thought. He might well have been asking himself why the polder that would not have been there without him, and in which he had invested so much sweat and so many sleepless nights, should now finally be named the "New Caroline Polder" after one of the princesses of the ruling houses; but it was so; the name stood there on every relevant document, on some even in red Gothic letters. Then, looking up, he saw two labourers with their farm tools coming towards him, one some twenty paces behind the other. "Wait, can't you!" he heard the trailing one call out; but the other, standing by a track that led down to the polder, called back: "Some other time, Jens! It's late now; I've got to spread the clay from the ditches!"

"Where?"

"Just here, in the Hauke Haien Polder!"

He shouted it aloud as he hurried down the track as though the whole marshland lying below were meant to hear. To Hauke it was as if he heard his own fame proclaimed; he raised himself in the stirrups, spurred his grey, and gazed steadily out over the wide landscape that lay to his left. "Hauke Haien Polder," he repeated quietly; it sounded as if it could never be called anything else! Let them defy him as much as they wished, but there was no avoiding his name; the princess's name – wouldn't that soon be mouldering in the old documents? – The grey galloped proudly along; but the words still rang in his ears: "Hauke Haien Polder! Hauke Haien Polder!" In his mind the new dyke almost grew to be the eighth wonder of the world; there was nothing like it in the whole of Friesland! He checked the grey to a prancing gait; he felt as though he stood in the midst of all the Friesian people; he towered a full head above them, his eyes passing over them keenly and compassionately.

Three years had passed since the dyking of the polder; the new dyke had proved itself, the repair costs had been only a trifle; in the polder white clover was now in flower nearly everywhere and to anyone who walked across the sheltered pastures the summer wind carried dense clouds of sweet scent. The time had now come to convert all the hitherto nominal shares in the polder into actual shares and to distribute these to all the owners accordingly. Hauke had not been slow to acquire some further new shares beforehand; Ole Peters had grimly held back and none of the new polder belonged to him. The division of shares had also not been without its frustrations and disputes, but it had nevertheless been completed; this day too lay behind the dykemaster.

* *

From that time on Hauke lived a solitary life fulfilling his duties as farmer and dykemaster and towards those who were closest to him; old friends had passed away and he was not the person to make new ones. But under his roof there was a calm which even the quiet child did not disturb; the child spoke little, the constant questions that are typical of lively children seldom came, and when they did, the person asked found them difficult to answer; but her lovely, simple little face almost always bore an expression of contentment. She had two playmates; they were enough for her: when she wandered over the earthwork of the farmstead the golden-haired dog that had been rescued was always jumping around her, and whenever the dog was about little Wienke was not far away either. Her second playmate was a black-headed gull. The dog was called Pearl and the gull Claus.

Claus had been brought to the farmstead by a very old soul: at the age of eighty Trin' Jans had no longer been able to manage on her own in her cottage on the dyke; it had then been Elke's wish to have her grandfather's aged housemaid spend a few quiet evenings with them and to offer her a home for the rest of her days, and so, with some pressure from Hauke and herself, she had been brought to the farm and accommodated in the small north-west room of the new barn which the dykemaster had had to build some years ago next to the main farmhouse as part of the expansion of his business. A couple of the servant-girls had been given their room next to her and were therefore on hand for the old woman at nights. Round the walls she had her household belongings: a strongbox made of hardwood from sugar chests, above it two coloured pictures of her dead son, a long-since unused spinning wheel and a spotless curtained bed, before which stood a crudely made footstool covered with the white fur of the late Angora cat. But she had also possessed something living and she had brought it with her: Claus the seagull had attached itself to her for some years now and had been fed by her; it did, however, fly southwards with the other gulls when winter arrived, and only returned when the wormwood bloomed on the shore.

The barn was somewhat lower down the earthwork than the main house; from her window the old woman could not see the sea for the dyke. "You're keeping me cooped up here like a prisoner, dykemaster!" she grumbled one day when Hauke came to see her, and pointed her crooked finger towards the fens which were spread out below. "Where's Jeverssand then? Over there beyond the red ox or beyond the black one?"

"Why do you want to see Jeverssand?" asked Hauke.

"Not so much Jeverssand!" muttered the old woman; "I just want to see the place where my son was taken to meet his Maker!"

"If you want to see it," replied Hauke, "you'll have to go up and sit under the ash tree; from there you can see the whole sea!"

"Oh yes," said the old woman; "yes, if I had your young legs, dykemaster!"

For a long time that was all the thanks the dykemaster's household received for their kindness to her; but then there was a sudden change. One morning Wienke's small head peeped in at her through the half-open door. "Well?" said the old woman who sat on her wooden stool with her hands folded, "What have you come for then?"

The child said nothing but came closer and did not stop staring at her with her calm eyes.

"Aren't you the dykemaster's child?" Trin' Jans asked her, and as the child lowered her head as though nodding in agreement, she continued: "Come and sit here on my footstool! It used to be an Angora cat – as big as that! But your father beat him to death. If it was still alive, you could ride on it."

Silently Wienke fixed her gaze on the white skin; then she kneeled down and began to stroke it with her small hands as children do to a live cat or dog. "Poor cat!" she said, and continued to caress it.

"There," said the old woman after a while, "that'll do for now; but you can sit on him now if you like; perhaps that's really why your father beat it to death!" Then she lifted the child up into the air by both her arms and sat her down firmly on the footstool. But as the child just sat there, neither speaking nor moving, her eyes never leaving the old woman, she began to shake her head.

"You're punishing him, O God! Oh yes, You're punishing him!" she murmured, but pity for the child seemed to overcome her; her bony hand stroked the child's wispy hair and the expression in the little girl's eyes suggested that it pleased her.

From then on Wienke went every day to see the old woman in her room. Of her own accord she was soon sitting on the Angora footstool, and Trin' Jans would give her scraps of meat and bread of which she always had a supply, and got her to throw them onto the floor; then the gull, squawking and with wings out-stretched, would come out from some corner of the room and set upon them. The child was startled at first by the huge raging bird and cried out; but it was soon like a familiar game, and she only had to put her small head round the door for the bird to dart towards her and perch on her head or shoulder until the old woman came to help her and the feeding could begin. Trin' Jans, who until then had not been able to stand anyone even stretching a hand towards Claus, now watched patiently as the child stead-ily won the bird over for herself. It willingly let her catch it; she carried it around everywhere and wrapped it in her apron, and when, out on the earthwork, the little golden dog scampered round her and jumped up jealously at the bird, she would cry out: "Not you, not you, Pearl!" and with her small arms lift the seagull so high in the air that, freeing itself, it would fly off screeching over the earthwork, and the dog would now try to take its place in her arms by jumping and nuzzling up to her.

If Hauke's and Elke's eyes should chance on this strange quadri-folium held on the same stem only by a common need, an affec-tionate glance would be cast towards their child; but once they had turned away, their faces retained only an expression of the sorrow that they carried away in their hearts, for the redeeming word had not yet been spoken between them. Then one summer morning, when Wienke was sitting with the old woman and both the animals on the large stones in front of the barn door, both her parents went by, the dykemaster leading his horse with the reins tucked over his arm; he was going to ride up onto the dyke and had fetched the horse in from the fen; his wife had slipped her arm into his as they crossed the earthwork. The sun shone warmly; it was almost sultry, and from time to time a gust of wind came from the south-south-east. The child might have become uncomfortable where she was sitting. "Wienke wants to come too!" she cried, brushing the seagull off her lap and reaching for her father's hand.

"Come on then!" he said.

But Elke cried: "In this wind? She'll be blown away!"

"I'll hold on to her; today we've got warm air and choppy water, so she can see it dancing."

Elke ran into the house and fetched a small headscarf and cap for her child. "But there's bad weather on the way," she said; "you'd better be off, and get back soon!"

Hauke laughed. "We won't get caught!" He lifted the child up to him and onto the saddle. Frau Elke remained standing on the earthwork for a while, her hand shading her eyes, watching them ride down along the path and up towards the dyke; Trin' Jans sat on the stone and muttered something incomprehensible through her withered lips.

The child lay motionless in her father's arm; it was as if she found it difficult to breathe in the heavy, thundery air; he inclined his head towards her. "Are you all right, Wienke?" he asked.

The child looked at him for a moment. "Father," she said, "you can do that! You can do everything, can't you?"

"What is it I can do, Wienke?"

But she did not say anything; she seemed not to have understood her own question.

It was high tide. When they arrived on the dyke the sun's reflection on the broad expanse of water shone into their eyes, a squall made the waves swirl up high into the air and others followed, crashing onto the shore; Wienke clasped her small hands in fear round her father's fist which, with a tug on the reins, caused the grey to start to one side. The pale blue eyes looked up at Hauke in confused fright. "The water, father! The water!" she cried.

He freed himself gently and said: "Quiet now, child, you're with your father; the water's not going to hurt you!"

She brushed the pale blond hair away from her brow and dared to look at the sea again. "It won't hurt me," she said, trembling; "No, tell it that it mustn't hurt us; you can do that, and then it won't hurt us!"

"I can't do that, child," replied Hauke in a serious tone; "but the dyke we're riding on, it's protecting us, and it was your father's idea and he had it built."

Her eyes looked at him as if she had not quite understood what he had said; then she hid her noticeably small head in her father's wide coat.

"Why are you hiding, Wienke?" he whispered to her; "are you still afraid?" And a trembling little voice came from the folds of his coat. "Wienke doesn't want to see; but you can do anything, father, can't you?"

Distant thunder rolled towards them on the wind. "Aha," exclaimed Hauke, "it's coming!" and he turned his horse about. "We'd better be getting on home to your mother!"

The child took a deep breath; but not until they had reached the earthwork and the house did she raise her head from her father's breast. And when Frau Elke had removed her cap and scarf inside the house, she stood quiet as a lamb in front of her mother. "Well, Wienke," said Elke, shaking her gently, "did you like all that water?"

But the child just opened her eyes wide. "It can talk," she said; "Wienke is afraid!"

"It can't talk; it just rushes and roars!"

The child stared vacantly. "Does it have legs?" she asked again. "Can it get over the dyke?"

"No, Wienke; your father makes sure of that, he's the dyke-master."

"Yes," said the child with a weak smile, clapping her small hands together. "Father can do anything – anything!" Then turning away from her mother, she suddenly cried: "Let Wienke go to Trin' Jans, she's got red apples!"

And Elke opened the door and let the child go out. After she had closed it, she looked up at her husband with an expression of deepest sorrow in her eyes which up until then had brought him only encouragement and comfort.

He took her hand and squeezed it as if there were no need for further words between them; but she said softly: "No, Hauke, let me speak: the child I bore you after years of marriage will always remain a child. Oh dear God! she's simple-minded; I have to say it, just this once, in front of you."

"I've known it for a long time," said Hauke and tightly held his wife's hand which she wanted to withdraw.

"So we're just as alone as ever we were," she continued.

But Hauke shook his head. "I love her and she throws her little arms round me and presses herself hard against my breast; I wouldn't be without that for all the treasures on earth!"

His wife gazed sombrely in front of her. "But why?" she said; "What have I, the poor mother, done to deserve this?"

"Yes, Elke, I've asked the same question of the One who alone can know; but you know that the Almighty doesn't give us human beings an answer – perhaps because we wouldn't comprehend it."

He had grasped his wife's other hand and pulled her gently to him. "Don't let yourself be put off loving your child as you do, Elke; you can be sure she understands!"

Elke threw herself into her husband's arms and cried until she could cry no more and she was no longer alone with her sorrow. Then she suddenly smiled up at him; and after clasping his hands tightly she ran outside, fetched Wienke from old Trin' Jans' room, put her on her lap and cuddled and kissed her until the little girl stammered: "Mother, my dear mother!"

❖ ❖

So they lived quietly together on the dykemaster's farmstead; much would have been missing if the child had not been there.

The summer drew gradually to a close; the migratory birds had passed over, the sky no longer contained lark song, and only from the barns, where these birds pecked for grains of corn during threshing, could a few of them occasionally be heard as they flew off with shrill cries; a hard frost had already set in. One afternoon in the kitchen of the main house, old Trin' Jans sat on the wooden step of a staircase which ran up into the loft next to the open brick hearth. During the past few weeks she seemed to have come to life again; now she liked to come into the kitchen sometimes and watch Elke busy at work; nothing more had been said about her legs not being able to get her there since the day little Wienke had tugged her all the way by her apron. The child was kneeling beside her, staring with her tranquil eyes at the flames that flickered up from the open hearth; one of her hands clasped the old woman's arm, the other rested in her own pale blond hair. Trin' Jans was telling her a story: "Do you know," she said, "I used to be in service with your great-grandfather as a housemaid and had to feed the pigs; he was wiser than them all – now once, it was a terribly long time ago now, one evening when the moon was shining they had closed the seaward sluice and she couldn't get back to the sea. Oh, how she cried and tore at her hard bristly hair with her fishy hands! Yes, child, I saw it and heard her crying myself! The ditches between the fens were all full of water and the moon shone down on them so that they gleamed like silver, and she swam out of one ditch into the next and lifted her arms and beat the things she had instead of hands together – you could hear the clapping a long way off – as though she wanted to pray; but, child, these creatures can't pray. I sat by the door on a couple of beams which had been delivered for building and looked right out across the fens; and the mermaid was still swimming about in the ditches and when she lifted her arms they too glittered like silver and diamonds in the moonlight. In the end I lost sight of her, and the wild geese and gulls, which I hadn't heard all this time, flew piping and cackling again through the air."

The old woman fell silent; the child had latched onto a word. "Could she pray?" she asked. "Could she? Who was it?"

"Child," said the old woman, "it was a mermaid; they are monsters who cannot be blessed."

"Not blessed!" repeated the child, and her small chest heaved a deep sigh as if she had understood the words.

"Trin' Jans!" came a deep voice from the kitchen door, and the old woman started slightly. It was the dykemaster Hauke Haien, leaning against the doorpost. "What's this you're telling the child? Haven't I instructed you to keep your fairy tales to yourself, or to save them for the geese and the chickens?"

The old woman gave him a dark look and pushed the child away. "They're not fairy tales," she mumbled to herself, "my great-uncle told them to me."

"Your great-uncle, Trin'? You said just now you had seen it all for yourself."

"What's that matter!" said the old woman; "you wouldn't believe it anyway, Hauke Haien; you want to make my great-uncle out to be a liar!" She moved closer to the hearth and stretched out her hands over the flames in the open grate.

The dykemaster cast a glance towards the window; it was only just beginning to get dark outside. "Come, Wienke!" he said, pulling his retarded child to him; "come with me, I'll show you something outside, from the top of the dyke! Only we need to go on foot – the horse is at the blacksmith's." Then he went with the child into the living room where Elke wrapped thick woollen scarves round the child's neck and shoulders; soon afterwards the father walked with her along the old dyke northwestwards, past Jeverssand to where the mudflats stretched far and wide, almost limitless.

Sometimes he carried her, sometimes she held his hand; gradually dusk fell; in the distance everything disappeared in mist and haze. But there before them, as far as the eye could see, the invisible swelling currents of water had split the ice, and, just as Hauke Haien had first seen it in his youth, out of the fissures as before, the mists rose like billowing smoke, in which a line of weird droll figures jumped against one another once more, bowing and scraping and suddenly expanding in a terrifying manner.

The child clung fearfully to her father, covering her face with his hand. "The sea-devils!" she whispered, trembling, between his fingers, "the sea-devils!"

He shook his head. "No, Wienke, neither mermaids nor sea-devils, there are no such things; who told you about them?"

She looked quietly up at him; but she did not answer. He lovingly stroked her cheeks. "Just have another look!" he said, "they're just poor hungry birds! Look how that big one's now spreading its wings; they're catching the fish which come up in those cracks where the mist is rising."

"Fish," repeated Wienke.

"Yes child, they're all living creatures, just as we are; there is nothing else; but God is everywhere!"

Little Wienke gazed fixedly at the ground and held her breath; it was as though she were staring, terrified, into an abyss. Perhaps it only seemed so; her father watched her for a long while, then bent down and looked into her face; but it contained not a flicker from her impenetrable soul. He lifted her into his arms and pushed her tiny frozen hands into one of his thick woollen gloves. "There, my Wienke" – but the child could not recognise the tone of deep affection in his words – "there, warm yourself against me! You are our child after all, our only one. You love us . . .!"

The man's voice broke; but the child gently pressed her little head into his rough beard.

So they went peacefully home.

✽ ✽

In the New Year the house had again been beset with worry; the dykemaster contracted marsh fever; he too came close to his grave, and when he had recovered through Frau Elke's nursing and care, he scarcely seemed to be the same man. He was mentally as well as physically exhausted, and Elke noticed with concern how easily satisfied he was all the time. However, towards the end of March he felt a need to mount his grey and for the first time to ride along his new dyke again; it was in the afternoon, and the sun which had been shining earlier had long since hidden itself again behind a dull haze.

There had been a couple of high tides in the winter; but they had not amounted to very much. Over on the other shore a flock of sheep had been drowned on a hallig and part of the foreland swept away, but on this side there had been no damage to the new polder worth mentioning. On the previous night, however, a fiercer storm had raged, and now the dykemaster needed to go out himself and inspect everything with his own eyes. He had already ridden round the new dyke from its south-east corner and found it all in good order; but when he arrived at the north-east corner, at the spot where the new dyke joined the old, he found that although the former was undamaged, where previously the watercourse had reached the old dyke and then run along by the side of it a large area of turf had been destroyed and ripped away, and a hollow gouged into the body of the dyke by the tide, which moreover exposed a maze of mouse-holes. Hauke dismounted and examined the damage at close quarters: the mouse-holes appeared without doubt to continue into the dyke, although to what extent could not be seen.

He was deeply alarmed; all this should have been taken care of during the building of the new dyke; but as it had been overlooked at the time, it had to be put right now! – The cattle were not yet out on the fens, for the grass was unusually late; wherever he looked it appeared bleak and desolate. He remounted and

100

rode back and forth along the shore: it was low tide and he saw clearly how the incoming current had again carved a bed for itself in the mud and was now striking against the old dyke from the north-west; the new dyke, as far as it was being struck, had been able to withstand the impact with its more gentle slope.

A mountain of new torments and work rose up in the dyke-master's mind; the old dyke had not only to be strengthened at this spot, but also its shape made more like that of the new one; and above all, the watercourse which had reappeared had to be treated as dangerous and diverted by new dams or brushwood groynes. Once again he rode along the new dyke to its far north-west corner, then back again, his eyes constantly fixed on the recently channelled bed of the watercourse which stood out quite clearly to one side of him in the exposed mudflat. The grey strained forward and snorted and pounded the ground with its forehoofs; but the rider reined it back, he wanted to ride slowly, and he wanted to control the inner torment which grew wilder within him.

If a storm tide were to come again – a tide as in 1655 when countless people and property had been engulfed – suppose it came again, as it already had done, more than once! The rider shuddered with horror: the old dyke – it would not withstand the blows that would be hurled against it! What then, what would happen then? Only one thing, there would perhaps be only one way to save the old polder and the lives and the property of the people upon it. Hauke felt his heart stop, his usually steady head reeled; he did not say it, but within him it spoke clearly enough: your polder, the Hauke Haien Polder, would have to be sacrificed and the new dyke breached!

In his mind he already saw the surging high tide breaking through the dyke and covering the grass and clover with its salty spume and spray. A spur shot into the flanks of the grey, and neighing loudly it flew along the top of the dyke and down the narrow track towards the dykemaster's earthwork.

He arrived home with his mind full of innermost horror and chaotic plans. He threw himself into his armchair, and when Elke entered the room with their daughter he stood up again and picked up the child and kissed her; then he shooed the little golden dog away with a few light taps. "I've got to go up to the inn again!" he said, taking his cap off the door-hook on which he had only just hung it.

His wife looked at him anxiously. "What are you going to do there? It'll soon be evening, Hauke!"

"About the dykes!" he murmured to himself. "I'm meeting some dyke commissioners there."

She followed after him squeezing his hand, for as he was speaking he was already on his way out of the door. Hauke Haien, who had previously always made his own decisions, now eagerly sought a word of advice from those whom he had formerly considered hardly worth consulting. In the parlour he met Ole Peters with three other dyke commissioners and a man from the polder sitting together round a card table.

"Just come in from out there, dykemaster?" said Ole Peters, picking up the partly-dealt cards and throwing them down again.

"Yes, Ole," replied Hauke; "I was out there; things look bad."

"Bad? – No, it might take a few hundred turfs and some straw-laying, that's all; I was there this afternoon too."

"We won't get off so cheaply, Ole," replied the dykemaster, "the watercourse is back, and even if it doesn't strike the old dyke from the north now, it's certainly striking it from the north-west!"

"You ought to have left it where you found it," said Ole drily.

"What you mean," retorted Hauke, "is that the new polder doesn't concern you, and therefore shouldn't exist. But that's your own fault! If we have to construct brushwood groynes to protect the old dyke, the income from the fresh clover gained by the new one will more than cover the cost!"

"What's that you're saying, dykemaster?" exclaimed the commissioners. "Brushwood groynes? How many then? You love to do things the most expensive way!"

The cards lay undisturbed on the table. "Let me tell you something, dykemaster," said Ole Peters, leaning forward on his elbows; "the new polder which you foisted on us is devouring us all! Everyone's still struggling to bear the heavy cost of your wide dykes; now the new dyke's eating up the old one, and we're supposed to renew it! – Luckily it's not too bad; it's held this time and will go on holding! Just get on your grey again in the morning and take another look at it!"

Hauke had come here from the peace of his house; behind the

fairly restrained words he had just heard – he could not mistake it – lay a tenacious resistance; he felt as though he lacked his old strength to fight against it. "I'll do as you advise, Ole," he said; "only I fear I'll find the same as I saw today."

A disturbed night followed this day; Hauke tossed and turned on his pillows. "What's the matter?" asked Elke whom worry for her husband had kept awake. "If something's on your mind, tell me; we've always confided in each other!"

"It's nothing, Elke! he replied. "Repairs are needed to the dyke and sluices; you know how I always think about these things at night." He said no more; he wanted to remain free to act as he thought fit; his wife's clear judgment and strong spirit were a hindrance he instinctively avoided in his present weak state.

The following morning when he rode up once more onto the dyke, the world was a different one from that of the previous day; it was low tide again, but the day was still short of its peak and the rays of the bright spring sun fell almost vertically onto the vast mudflats; white gulls glided serenely back and forth, and unseen above them, high under the azure of the sky, the larks sang their eternal melody. Hauke, who was unaware how Nature can deceive us with her charms, stood at the north-west corner of the dyke and searched for the bed of the new watercourse that had so shocked him the previous day; but in the light that flooded down from the overhead sun he could not see it at first. Not until he had shaded his eyes against the blinding light did he see it unmistakably; but the shadows of the previous day's twilight must have deceived him, for hardly a trace of it showed now; the exposed mouse colony must have caused more damage to the dyke than the tide. Of course something had to be done about it, but through careful digging-out and, as Ole Peters had said, new turfs and a few yards of straw-covering, the damage could be made good.

"It wasn't as bad as that," he said to himself, relieved, "you made a fool of yourself yesterday!" – He called a meeting of the dyke commissioners and the work was put in hand without any opposition – something that had never happened before. The dykemaster seemed to feel a strengthening calm spreading through his still weakened body, and some weeks later everything was satisfactorily carried out.

The year moved on, but the further it went and the more the newly laid turf showed green through the covering of straw, the more anxiously Hauke walked or rode past this spot. He would avert his gaze or ride on the landward side of the dyke; several times, when he should have gone to the spot, he had had his already saddled horse led back to the stables; at other times, when he had no business there at all, he had suddenly made his way to the place on foot so that he might get away from his earthwork quickly and unseen; sometimes he had even turned back, feeling unable to set eyes on the uncanny place again. In the end he would have liked to rip it all apart with his own bare hands, for this section of the dyke stood there before him like a pang of conscience which had taken shape outside his mind. And yet he was now quite unable to lay hands on it; and to no one, not even to his wife, could he talk about it. And so September came; a moderate storm had raged during the night and had finally veered to the north-west. On the following morning, at low tide, beneath a leaden sky, Hauke rode out along the dyke, and when his eyes combed the mudflats the sight suddenly struck him; there, coming in from the north-west, he saw it again, more cleanly and deeply cut into the mud, the ghostly new bed of the watercourse; and however much he strained his eyes it was still there.

When he arrived home, Elke seized his hand. "What's wrong, Hauke?" she said when she looked into his sombre face, "not new mischief? We're so happy now; I feel that you've made your peace with them all now!"

In response to this remark he was incapable of putting his confused fear into words.

"No, Elke," he said, "no one's against me; it's just that it's a responsible office, having to protect the community against the Lord God's sea."

He broke away to avoid any further questions from his beloved wife. He went into the stable and the barn as if he needed to inspect everything there; but he saw nothing of his surroundings; his only concern was to still the nagging of his conscience and to convince himself that it was no more than a morbidly exaggerated fear.

'The year I'm telling you about,' my host the schoolmaster said

104

after a short while, 'was the year 1756, which will never be forgotten in these parts; it brought a death to Hauke Haien's house. At the end of September Trin' Jans, now nearly ninety, lay dying in the small bedroom that had been made up for her in the barn. She had been propped up by cushions, as she had wished, and she could see out through the small leaded windows into the distance; there must have been a thinner layer of air in the sky lying over a thicker one, for there was a kind of mirage as reflection at this moment lifted the sea like a glittering strip of silver above the ridge of the dyke so that it shimmered dazzlingly into the room; even the southern point of Jeverssand was visible.

Little Wienke cowered at the foot of the bed and tightly held one of her father's hands as he stood beside her. Death was just beginning to engrave its image on the dying woman's face, and the child held her breath as she stared at the uncanny and to her incomprehensible transformation that was occurring in the unlovely yet familiar features.

"What's she doing? What is it, father?" she whispered fearfully, digging her fingernails into her father's hand.

"She's dying!" said the dykemaster.

"Dying!" repeated the child, and seemed to lapse into confused thought.

But the old woman moved her lips once more. "Jens! Jens!" And a shriek, like a cry of distress, burst from her mouth and her bony arms stretched towards the glittering reflection of the sea outside. "Help me! Help me! You're above the water . . . God have mercy on the others!"

Her arms fell back, a soft creak of the bed was audible; she had ceased to live.

The child gave a deep sigh and her pale eyes glanced up at her father. "Is she still dying?" she asked.

"For her it is over!" said the dykemaster and took the child in his arms. "She's a long way from us now, with God."

"With God!" repeated the child and paused for a moment as if she must reflect on the words. "Is that good, to be with God?"

"Yes, it's the best of all." – But the last words of the dying woman weighed heavily on Hauke's soul. "God have mercy on the others!" the words sounded quietly within him. "What did the old witch mean? Are the dying prophets?"

Soon after Trin' Jans had been buried up by the church, people began to talk more and more about all kinds of misfortunes and strange insects that were said to have frightened the people of North Friesland; and it was certainly true that on Mid-Lent Sunday the golden cockerel on the church spire had been brought down by a whirlwind; it was also true that in midsummer huge swarms of flies and other troublesome insects descended from the sky like snow, so that people were unable to open their eyes, and afterwards they lay almost a hand's breadth deep on the fens, and no one had seen anything like it before. But when at the end of September when the head-farmhand had driven to the market in town with corn, and the maidservant, Ann Grete, with butter, they both climbed down from their wagon on their return home with deathly-white faces. "What is it? What's the matter?" cried the other maids who had run outside when they heard the rumbling of the wagon.

Ann Grete in her travel attire breathlessly entered the spacious kitchen. "Well, come on, tell us then!" cried the maids again, "where's disaster struck this time?"

"Oh, may the dear Lord protect us!" cried Ann Grete. "You know old Mary over there, the other side of the water, from the red brick farmhouse, well as usual, we all went together with our butter to stand at the corner by the pharmacy, she told me all about it, and Iven Johns told us too, 'There's going to be a disaster!' he said; 'a disaster over the whole of North Friesland; believe me, Ann Gret!' And" – she lowered her voice – "there's something not quite right about that dykemaster's grey after all!"

"Sh! sh!" went the other maids.

"I know, I know, but it doesn't worry me! Over there on the other side it's even worse than here! Not just flies and vermin, blood also fell from the sky like rain; and when the pastor went to his washbasin the next Sunday morning there were five skulls the size of peas in it, and everyone came to see; in August there were horrible red-headed caterpillars crawling everywhere, eating up corn and flour and bread and whatever they could find, and even fire couldn't destroy them!"

The speaker suddenly fell silent; none of the maidservants had noticed that their mistress had come into the kitchen. "What's this you're talking about?" she asked. "Never let the master hear that!" And as they all now wanted to tell her the tale: "There's no need, I've heard quite enough already; get on with your work, more good will come of that!" Then she took Ann Grete with her into the living room and went over the accounts for the day's business at the market.

Thus in the dykemaster's household there was no place for superstitious gossip; but in the others, the longer the evenings became, the more the gossip took hold. A dark cloud seemed to hang over everyone, and people were saying secretly to themselves that a catastrophe, a terrible one, would strike North Friesland.

It was All Saints' Eve, in October. All day a wind had raged from the south-west; in the evening a half-moon stood in the sky, dark-brown clouds raced across it, and shadows and dim light flew in confusion over marsh and polder; the storm was gathering. In the dykemaster's living room the remains of the evening meal had not yet been cleared away; the farmhands had been sent to the stable to attend to the cattle, the maidservants around the house and up into the lofts to check that doors and shutters were firmly closed so that the storm could not sweep in and cause damage. Inside the house Hauke stood next to his wife by the window; he had only just swallowed down his supper, having been out on the dyke. He had tramped out on foot early in the afternoon. At places where the dyke appeared weak he had had sharpened stakes and sacks of clay or earth stockpiled; he had posted men everywhere to ram in the stakes and pack down the sacks as soon as the tide began to harm the dyke; he had posted the most men at the north-west corner, where the old and the new dyke met; only in an emergency were they permitted to leave their appointed stations. Having arranged all this, he had arrived home, wet and windswept, scarcely a quarter of an hour previously, and now, listening to the blasts of the wind which made the leaded window panes rattle, he stared blankly out into the wild night; the wall clock behind its glass was just striking eight. The child, standing next to her mother, shuddered and hid her head in her mother's skirt. "Claus!" she cried, sobbing, "where is my Claus?"

She had good cause to ask, for this year as last the gull had not set out on its winter journey. The father ignored the question; but the mother lifted the child up into her arms. "Your Claus is in the barn," she said; "he's warm sitting there."

"Why?" said Wienke, "is that good?"

"Yes, that's good."

The master of the house remained standing by the window. "It won't do, Elke!" he said. "Call one of the maids; the storm will blow in the panes, the shutters must be bolted to!"

The mistress's words sent the maid running outside; from inside the room her skirts could be seen flying about in the wind; but when she released the clasps, the storm ripped the shutter from her hands and slammed it against the window so that a few splintered panes of glass flew into the room and one of the candles went out, smoking. Hauke himself had to go outside to help, and only after much effort were the shutters gradually secured in front of the windows. When they heaved open the door to re-enter the house, a blast of wind followed them in, making the glass and silverware clash together in the wall cabinet; the beams of the house shook and creaked above their heads as if the storm wanted to rip the roof from the walls. But Hauke did not come back into the room; Elke heard him striding across the threshing floor of the barn towards the stable. "The grey! The grey, John! Hurry!" she heard him call; then he returned to the room, his hair dishevelled, his grey eyes burning. "The wind's veered!" he exclaimed – "to the north-west, on a half spring-tide! It's more than a wind – we've never had a storm like this!"

Elke had gone deathly white. "And you've got to go out again?"

He grasped both her hands, pressing them convulsively in his. "I have to, Elke."

She raised her dark eyes slowly towards him, and for a few seconds they looked at each other; yet it was like an eternity.

"Yes, Hauke," she said, "I know you have to!"

There was a sound of trotting outside the door. She threw her arms about his neck, and for a moment it seemed as if she could not let him go; but even that was only for a moment. "This is *our* struggle!" said Hauke; "you're safe here; no flood has ever reached up to this house. And pray to God that He's with me too!"

Hauke wrapped himself in his cape, and Elke took a scarf and wound it carefully round his neck; she wanted to say something but her trembling lips prevented her.

Outside the house the grey's whinny sounded in the howling of the storm like the blast of a trumpet. Elke had gone outside with her husband; the old ash tree was creaking as though it were about to split apart. "Quick, mount, sir!" shouted the farmhand, "the grey's near wild; the reins might snap." Hauke threw his arms round his wife. "I'll be home again before dawn!"

He was immediately in the saddle. The animal reared with its forehoofs in the air, then, like a charger rushing into battle, it sped with its rider down the earthwork, out into the night and the howling storm. "Father! My father!" cried a child's anguished voice after him. "Dear father!"

In the darkness Wienke had run after them; but after only a hundred paces she stumbled over a mound of earth and fell to the ground.

The farmhand, Iven Johns, brought the crying child back to her mother, now leaning against the trunk of the ash whose branches were lashing about wildly in the air above her head, apparently staring absently into the darkness into which her husband had disappeared; and when the roar of the storm and the distant crashing of the waves ceased for a moment, she started with terror; she felt as if everything was now intent simply on destroying him, and when it had snatched him, silence would suddenly fall. Her knees trembled, the storm had loosened her hair and was playing with it. "Here's the child, ma'am!" shouted Johns; "Hold her tight!" And he pressed the child into her mother's arms.

"The child? – I'd forgotten you, Wienke!" she cried; "God forgive me!" Then she clasped the child to her breast as tightly as only love knows how and dropped to her knees with her to pray: "Dear God, and Jesus, let us not be widowed and orphaned! Protect him, dear God; only You and I, only we two know him." But the storm did not abate; it raged and thundered as though the whole world were about to perish in limitless commotion.

"Get into the house, ma'am!" said Johns. "Come!" And he helped them up and led them both towards the house and into the living room.

Dykemaster Hauke Haien raced on his grey towards the dyke. The narrow path was sodden, for the day before it had rained heavily, but the wet clinging clay appeared not to hinder the horse, it was as if it had firm summer ground under its hoofs. Clouds sped across the sky like a wild chase; below lay the immense marsh like an unrecognisable wilderness filled with restless shadows; from the water behind the dyke, more and more terribly, came a dull roar as if it were intent on devouring all before it. "Forward!" shouted Hauke. "We're in for our worst ride!"

A cry, as if from a dying creature, came from under the horse's hoofs. He tugged at the reins and looked around: to one side of him, close to the ground, half flying, half driven by the storm, struggled a flock of white gulls, cackling scornfully; they sought shelter inland. One of them – the moon appeared for a fleeting moment from behind the clouds – lay crushed on the track: it looked to the rider as if a red ribbon fluttered about its neck. "Claus!" he cried. "Poor Claus!"

Was it his child's bird? Had it recognised the rider and horse and tried to find shelter with them? – The rider did not know. "Forward!" he shouted again, and the grey had just raised its hoofs to ride on when the storm suddenly ceased; a deathly silence took its place, only for a second, then it returned with renewed fury; but the sound of voices and the barking of lost dogs had meanwhile struck the rider's ears, and when he turned his head towards his village he recognised, in the moonlight that had broken through the clouds, people bustling round fully laden wagons up on the earthworks and in front of the houses; he saw yet more wagons, as if fleeing, being driven to safety towards the uplands; the bellowing of cattle which were also being driven up there out of the warm stables met his ears. "Thank God they're busy saving themselves and their cattle!" he shouted within himself; then with a fearful cry: "My wife! My child! – No, no, the water never reaches to the top of our earthwork!"

But the scene lasted only a moment; it passed like a fleeting vision.

A violent gust of wind came roaring in from the sea, and rider and horse fought their way against it up the narrow path towards the ridge of the dyke. When they were on top, Hauke forcefully

110

reined in his horse. But where was the sea? Where was Jeverssand? Where had the opposite shore gone? – He saw only mountains of water before him which towered up menacingly towards the night sky and in the terrible twilight sought to roll one over the other, and one over the other crashed against the dry land. Crowned with white plumes they rolled in, roaring, as if the cries of every ferocious wild beast in the wilderness were contained within them. The grey stamped the ground with its forehoofs and snorted with its nostrils into the tumult; it felt to the rider that here all mortal power ended; that now the forces of darkness, of death, of nothingness, were about to descend.

Then he reflected: it was just a storm tide after all; only he had never before seen a storm such as this; his wife, his child, they were both safe there on the high earthwork in the solid house; and his dyke – what pride swelled up in his breast – the Hauke Haien Dyke, as people called it, it would show them now how dykes should be built!

But – what was this? He stopped at the corner between the two dykes; where were the men he had posted here, who should have been keeping watch? – He looked northwards along the line of the old dyke, for there too he had posted one or two men. On neither dyke could he see a single soul; he rode out a short way, but still remained alone; only the wailing of the storm and the roaring of the sea from an immeasurable distance stunned his ears. He turned his horse about, returned to the deserted corner and let his eyes run along the ridge of his new dyke; he noticed distinctly how the waves rolled up the dyke more slowly and less forcefully there; it almost appeared as if it were a different sea. "That will certainly hold!" he murmured, and laughing joy rose in him.

But his joy ceased when his glance reached further along the line of his dyke: at the north-west corner – what was that? A dark mass was swarming about; he saw it moving hurriedly and urgently – without doubt, it was men! What were they up to, what were they doing to his dyke? – And the spurs were already into the flanks of his grey, and the animal flew with him towards them; the storm was broadside on; from time to time the wind gusted so fiercely that they were nearly blown off the dyke down into the new polder; but horse and rider knew where they were riding. Hauke had already made out that there were a good few dozen men there all working frantically together, and he could already see that a trench had been dug diagonally across the new dyke. He forcibly reined in his horse. "Stop!" he cried. "Stop! What in the devil's name are you doing?"

The men had ceased digging in terror at suddenly finding the dykemaster in their midst; the storm had carried his words towards them and he saw that several of them were struggling to answer; but he made out only their frantic gestures, for they all stood to his left and what they said was carried away by the wind, which here in the open frequently made the men reel against one another so that they huddled close together. Hauke's sharp eyes measured the newly dug trench and the level of the waves, which, in spite of the new dyke's shape, were breaking almost at the ridge, drenching horse and rider with spume. Just ten more minutes' work, he saw clearly, and the storm tide would break through the trench and the Hauke Haien Polder would be buried under the sea!

The dykemaster beckoned one of the men round to the other side of his horse. "Now, speak up!" he shouted. "What's going on here? What's the meaning of all this?"

"We've got to breach the new dyke, sir!" the workman shouted back, "to prevent the old one breaching!"

"Do what?"

"Breach the new dyke!"

"And flood the new polder? – What devil ordered you to do that?'

"No, sir, not a devil; the dyke commissioner, Ole Peters, has been here. He ordered it!"

Fury flashed in the rider's eyes. "Don't you know who I am?" he shouted. "Where I am, Ole Peters has no authority! Be off with you! Get back to where I put you!"

And as they hesitated he spurred his grey into their midst. "Be off! Damn the lot of you!"

"Watch what you're doing, sir!" cried a man from the group, thrusting his spade towards the maddened animal; but a thrashing hoof knocked the spade from his hand, another knocked him to the ground. Suddenly a cry rose from the rest of the group, a cry as only mortal terror can snatch from men's throats. In an instant everyone was paralysed, even the dykemaster and the grey; only

112

one of the men had moved to stretch out his arm like a signpost; he was pointing to the north-west corner of the two dykes, to the spot where the old met the new. Only the raging of the storm and the roar of the sea was to be heard. Hauke turned in his saddle: what was happening over there? His eyes widened. "My God! A breach! A breach in the old dyke!"

"Your fault, dykemaster!" cried a voice from the group. "Your fault! You'll answer before God's throne for this, you will!"

Hauke's angry red face had gone a deathly white; the moon which shone upon it could not add to its pallor, his arms hung limply, he hardly knew if he held the reins. But it was only a moment; he straightened himself in the saddle, a harsh groan escaped from his mouth; then he turned his horse without uttering a word, and the grey snorted and raced off eastwards with him along the dyke to the north-west corner. The rider's eyes darted everywhere; thoughts whirled in his head: what had he to answer for before God's throne? – The breaching of the new dyke? Perhaps they would have finished it if he had not ordered them to stop; but there was something else, it burned deep into his soul, he knew it only too well – last summer, if Ole Peters' wicked tongue had not held him back at that time – that was it! He alone had recognised the weakness in the old dyke; in spite of everything he should have pushed ahead with the new work. "I confess, O God," he suddenly cried out into the storm, "I have failed in the duties of my office!"

On his left, close to his horse's hoofs, the sea raged; in front of him, and now in complete darkness, lay the old polder with its earthworks and homesteads; the pale moonlight had disappeared completely; a single light penetrated the darkness. And it came as a warm comfort to the man's heart; it must be shining across from his own house, it was like a greeting to him from his wife and child. Thank God they were safe on the high earthwork! And certainly the others were already safe up there in the upland village; he had never before seen so many gleams of light shimmering from there; from high in the air too, it might well be coming from the church steeple, light was shining into the night. "They'll all be gone now, all of them!" said Hauke to himself; "to be sure, many a house on its earthwork will be left in ruins; terrible years lie ahead for the flooded fens, sluices will have to be repaired!

We'll have to endure it, and I'll help, I'll even help those who have wronged me; only, O Lord God, have mercy on us all!"

He glanced sidewards at the new polder; round it the sea foamed, but within it lay the stillness of night. An involuntary joy rose within the rider's breast: "The Hauke Haien Dyke, it will hold firm; and will still hold firm a hundred years from now!"

A thunderous roar at his feet roused him from these dreams; the grey refused to go on. What was it? The horse leapt back, and he felt it, a part of the dyke in front of him fell into the depths. He opened his eyes wide and cast all musing from his mind: he halted at the old dyke, on which the grey's forehoofs already rested. Instinctively he reined the horse back; the last blanket of cloud flew away from the moon and its mild light lit up the horror that, foaming and hissing before him, poured down into the old polder.

Hauke stared at it, stupefied; it was the Second Flood, to engulf man and beast. Light again flashed into his eyes; it was the same beam that he had made out earlier, still shining from his earthwork; his courage returned, and when he next looked down into the polder he saw clearly that only about a hundred paces' breadth had been flooded behind the swirling torrent of water that thundered down before him; beyond, he could clearly make out the road that led up to the dyke. But he saw even more: a wagon, no, a two-wheeled trap was racing up towards the dyke; a woman, and a child too, sat in it. And now – didn't he catch the yelping of a little dog on the stormwind? Almighty God! It was his wife, his child! They were already close and the foaming mass of water was surging towards them. A cry, a cry of despair broke from the rider's breast. "Elke!" he cried, "Elke! Back! Go back!"

But the storm and the sea were without mercy, their fury tore his words to shreds. The storm had seized his cape, it would soon have torn him from his horse; and the trap raced on without stopping towards the plunging torrent. Then he saw that his wife seemed to be holding up her arms to him. Had she recognised him? Had her longing for him, her fear for his life, driven her from the safety of her home? And now was she calling a last message to him? – The questions flashed through his mind; they remained without answers: from her to him, from him to her, all words were lost; only a roar as if the end of the world had come filled their ears and blocked out all other sound.

"My child! Oh Elke, Oh faithful Elke!" cried Hauke into the face of the storm. A large part of the dyke again then broke away in front of him into the depths and the sea thundered after it down into the polder; once more he saw the horse's head below and the wheels of the vehicle rising up out of the seething horror, then, swirling, sink beneath it. The staring eyes of the rider, who stood so alone on the top of the dyke, saw nothing more. "The end!" he said softly to himself; then he rode to the edge of the breach where below him the thunderous water was beginning to flood his village; he still saw the light shimmering from his house; it appeared lifeless to him. He straightened himself in the saddle and dug the spurs into the horse's flanks. The horse reared and almost toppled, but the rider's strength forced it down towards the water. "Forward!" he commanded once again, as he had so often done to urge it into a gallop. "Take me, Lord God; but have mercy on the others!"

Another jab of the spur; the horse's shrill cry rose above the noise of the storm and the thundering of the waves; then below, from out of the plunging water, a muffled sound, a brief struggle.

The moon shone brightly in the sky; but below on the dyke there was no living thing, only the wild water which had soon almost completely flooded the old polder. The earthwork of Hauke Haien's farmstead, however, still towered alone above the torrent, its gleam of light still shimmered, and from the uplands, where the houses gradually grew darker, the lonely light from the church steeple continued to throw its trembling light over the foaming waves.'

❊ ❊

The narrator fell silent. I reached for the filled glass which had stood for some time in front of me; but I did not raise it to my mouth; my hand remained resting on the table.

'That is the story of Hauke Haien,' my host began again. 'I've told it to the best of my knowledge. No doubt our dykemaster's housekeeper would have told you something quite different. Some even say that after the flood the bleached skeleton of the horse was to be seen again, as before, in the moonlight on Jevershallig; the whole village claims to have seen it. – But this much is true: Hauke

Haien and his wife and child perished in that flood; I have been unable to find their graves up there in the churchyard, the dead bodies will have been swept out to sea by the water retreating through the breach in the dyke, and will have gradually decomposed on the sea bed – so they have won their peace from their fellow men. But the Hauke Haien Dyke still stands today, after a hundred years, and if you ride into the town tomorrow, and don't mind the half-hour detour, you'll have it under the hoofs of your horse.

The thanks which Jewe Manners promised its builder from the grandchildren of his generation were, as you have seen, never forthcoming; for that's how things are, sir: they gave Socrates poison to drink and they nailed our Lord Jesus to the cross! It hasn't been so easy to do such things in recent times; but – we can still make a saint out of a tyrant or a wicked bull-necked priest, or a phantom out of an able man for the simple reason that he stood head and shoulders above the rest – that we can do every day.'

When the serious little man had said that, he stood up and listened to what was going on outside. 'It's changed out there now,' he said and pulled the woollen curtain back from the window; it was bright moonlight. 'Look,' he continued, 'the dyke committee's on its way back; but they're separating, they're going home – there must have been a breach over there on the other shore; the water level's fallen.'

I stood beside him and looked out; the windows here were above the ridge of the dyke; and it was as he had said. I picked up my glass and drank it. 'Many thanks for this evening!' I said; 'I think we can sleep in peace!'

'That we can,' replied the little man. 'I wish you a very good night!'

On my way out I met the dykemaster in the hallway; he had wanted to take home a map he had left behind in the parlour. 'It's all over!' he said. 'But I'm sure our schoolmaster's spun you a fine yarn; he belongs to the rationalists!'

'He seems to me a very sensible man!'

'Of course, of course, certainly; but you can't mistrust your own eyes; and over there on the other side, I said it would happen, the dyke has been breached!'

I shrugged my shoulders. 'We shall have to sleep on it! Good night, dykemaster!'

He laughed: 'Good night!'

The next morning, beneath a brilliant golden sun which had risen over widespread devastation, I rode along the Hauke Haien Dyke down to the town.

Notes

In the notes that follow I am greatly indebted to Karl Ernst Laage's commentary on *Der Schimmelreiter* in his edition of Storm (see Translator's Preface); and, for the information and sources provided in their editions of the Novelle, to Margaret L. Mare (Methuen, London, 1973) and Ingwert Paulsen Jr (Husum Druck- und Verlagsgesellschaft, Husum, 1994). I am also indebted to the notes and commentaries by Hans Wagener (*Erläuterungen und Dokumente,* Philipp Reclam, Stuttgart, 1976) and by Gerd Eversberg (*Königs Erläuterungen und Materialien,* C. Bange Verlag, Hollfeld, 1989).

Page 13: *old Frau Senator Feddersen.* Behind this figure lies Theodor Storm's maternal great-grandmother, Elsabe Fedderson, née Thomsen (1741-1829), whom he frequently visited as a boy and whose patrician house stood facing the small harbour in Husum, the small coastal town in the duchy of Schleswig that was his birthplace. Her husband, Jochim Christian Feddersen (1740-1801), was a Senator (Councillor) and prominent merchant of the town.

Page 13: *Leipzig Journal or Pappe's Hamburg Digest.* Two popular literary magazines of the beginning of the nineteenth century.

Page 13: *the truth of the following account.* Storm takes basic details of his plot from a story entitled *Der gespenstige Reiter* ('The Ghostly Rider'), first published in the weekly *Danziger Dampfboot* for 14 April 1838 and reprinted in the second volume of J.J. Pappe's annual digest of the same year, *Lesefrüchte vom Felde der neuesten Literatur des In- und Auslandes,* the version that Storm probably read. The narrator tells of seeing a ghostly rider on the banks of the Vistula in the region of Marlbork (Marienburg); see Afterword for further details. In old age Storm wrongly believed the story to have appeared before his great-grandmother's death in 1829.

Page 13: *the third decade of the present century.* The nineteenth century.

Page 13: *a North Friesian dyke.* The flat-ridged, earth dykes along the west coast of Schleswig-Holstein, based on Dutch designs to protect the land from storm tides from the North Sea, were about sixteen feet in height in the eighteenth and nineteenth centuries. They are much higher than this today and stretch some 80 miles on the mainland and 60 miles on the islands.

Page 13: *the desolate marsh*. The flat lowlands of the western coastal regions of Schleswig-Holstein with green pastures and solitary farms protected from the sea by the dykes: quite distinct from English 'marsh'. The marsh that the rider here sees, a joint product of river and sea, but almost wholly man-made, was extremely rich pasture land reclaimed from the sea by a dyking process that had been going on in the region for centuries.

Page 13: *North Sea tidal flats*. The Wattenmeer: a vast area of sand and mudflats exposed for many hours at low tide between the North Friesian Islands and the mainland coastline. The Wattenmeer with its islands and Halligen covers some 200,000 hectares. It is one of the largest continuous areas of mudflats in the world.

Page 13: *The Halligen and the other islands*. The North Friesian Islands off the west coast of Schleswig-Holstein. *Halligen* are small islands unprotected by dykes, some only a few feet above sea level. Today as in Storm's time they are crowned either by a single isolated house standing on an artificial earthwork (*Werft(e)*) or by a complex of houses on one or more earthworks; the complex sometimes includes a church that doubles as the local school (Hallig Gröde, for example, today possesses the smallest school in Germany with an average of only two pupils).

Page 14: *town*. Believed to be Husum. Theodor Storm in a letter to Gottfried Keller of 9 December 1887 described the setting of the Novelle simply as 'somewhere behind the dykes in the North Friesian marshland', and in a later letter to Ferdinand Tönnies of 7 April 1888 as 'a tale from the marshland'. Research has established that the author had in mind the more precise location of the Hattstedt marsh and its coastal region that lie to the north of Husum.

Page 15: *polder*. An area of fertile marshland reclaimed from the sea by dyking; known in North Friesland as a *Koog* or *Kog*.

Page 15: *Wehle*. A breach pond in marsh caused by the inrush of water through a breach in a dyke. Breach ponds of over thirty yards across have been known. The traces of such a pond, the Grosse Wehle, which was created in the Hattstedt marsh when its dyke was breached during the 'Christmas storm' of 1717, can still be seen today (see also note to page 105).

Page 15: *those low Friesian longhouses*. The typical North Friesian house is the long, low, thatched Utland house divided in the middle by a hall that separates the living quarters from the main work areas of threshing floor, barn and stables. The longer axes of such houses generally lie East-West so that their narrow gable-ends face the strong west winds rather than their much wider frontages. Their style reflects the flat landscape.

Page 15: *high earthworks.* The North Sea coast of Germany has many examples of settlements on round earthworks (*Werft(e)*), originally natural, but with many artificial additions and known locally in Low German as *Warften, Warfen* or *Wurten.* Some large earthworks are crowned by small villages, some by isolated farmsteads or longhouses. Various sizes of earthworks are to be found on the Halligen and marshlands and they vary in height up to about fifteen feet. In earlier times, before the building of dykes, they were the only protection against the sea.

Page 15: *it was an inn.* The model is believed to be the old thatch-roofed inn at Sterdebüll, north of Husum, which can still be seen to this day. Its design, appearance, height and location relative to the dyke are similar to the inn of the story. The present-day inn at Sterdebüll bears the name *Der Schimmelreiterkrug.* The inn is situated on level ground away from the dyke. Half its height extends above the dyke's ridge as here described by the rider.

Page 15: *Low German ... in use here alongside Friesian.* After the Reformation the use of the Friesian language declined in favour of Low German (Plattdeutsch) and High German, and by the seventeenth century it had already lost its position as the language of everyday life. The use of the language today has increased primarily through the promotion of the North Friesian Institute in Bredstedt.

Page 15: *Dykemaster and members of the dyke committee, and some landowners from these parts.* The office of *Deichgraf* (dykegrave; 'dyke-master' in the present translation) was established in North Friesland at the beginning of the seventeenth century and was modelled on the Dutch administrative system. The holder of the office was an elected official responsible for all matters concerning the dykes that protected his village and the surrounding lands. He was generally an influential landowner who could afford the expenses of his office and was able to exert the necessary authority within the community. A dyke committee, of which he was head and to which prominent men in the community were elected as commissioners, existed to assist him. Each commissioner was normally responsible for the supervision of an allocated section of the dyke, and landowners whose land was protected by it had a responsibility for its maintenance and upkeep in proportion to their landholding, often supplying farm- or day-labourers for this purpose. The old parishes in the area originally equated to the dyke administration areas, following the old North Friesian principle: 'No dyke without land, and no land without a dyke.'

Page 16: *over there, on the other side.* Storm probably had in mind the large island of Strand, or Old Nordstrand, just over a mile off the coast of Husum, which existed before the great storm of 1634 which devastated and considerably changed the coastline of North Friesland. In a letter dated 10 February 1885 to the wife of Deichbauinspektor Christian Hinrich Eckermann of Heide, a recognised authority on dykes at the time, Theodor Storm confirms his adoption of the former coastline for his Novelle: 'For a new work that is taking shape in my mind, I should like to have a sketch-map of the Nordstrand, Husum and Simonsberg area just as it was before the great storm of 1634. As I am referring to the old map that [your husband] recently showed me, perhaps he would allow me [...] to have it copied. Attention needs to be given to the location of the dykes and to place names [...].'

It is probable that the map referred to was that produced by the Husum cartographer Johannes Meyer, contained in Caspar Danckwerth's *Neue Landesbeschreibung der zwei Herzogtümer Schleswig und Holstein*, Schleswig, 1652 (see map on page 10).

Page 16: *the last century.* The eighteenth century.

Page 16: *in the year '17.* In an earlier draft of the story Storm had written 'thirteen years ago' at this point in the text. Given the period in which the story is being told, 'the third decade of the present century', there is no great storm recorded for 1817 in the region. The great 'Christmas Storm' of 24 December 1717, the worst in the eighteenth century, which devastated the entire coastline from the Netherlands to Denmark, is outside the frame of the narration.

Page 16: *Our schoolmaster.* The travel-writer Theodor Mügge, in his tale *Sam Wiebe* (1854), a picture of daily life in the marshland, provides a description of a type of schoolmaster common in the Hattstedt marsh region at the time, the *Wanderlehrer* (peripatetic teacher). The hero of the Novelle explains: 'Each family lives here alone in a farm on an earthwork. Where there's no village there's no school, so the schoolmaster walks from earthwork to earthwork. It happens sometimes that children from surrounding earthworks assemble together on one of them, and are taught for perhaps four to six weeks, until the teacher moves on to the next district to repeat the process. He travels and teaches like this for perhaps six months to a year, then returns to start the teaching over again.'

Such a teacher, Sievert Hansen from the 'Peterswarft' in the Hattstedt marsh, an intelligent man, 'somewhat hunched', has been linked with Storm's schoolmaster.

Page 17: *In the middle of the last century.* Around 1750.

Page 17: *Hans Mommsen from Fahretoft.* Dykemaster and land survey-or (1735-1811); the son of a marshland farmer who lived in Fahretoft north-west of Husum between Bredstedt and Niebüll. A self-taught mathematician of great academic and practical ability and a maker of clocks and measuring instruments, he inherited the post of dykemaster after his father's death in 1770. There are many parallels between aspects of Mommsen's early life and learning and the descriptions of the boy-hood of Storm's dykemaster.

Page 17: *fens.* Tracts of marshland enclosed by drainage ditches.

Page 18: *Euclid.* Greek mathematician of Alexandria (c.330-c.260 BC), author of *Elements* which sets out the principles of geometry, a subject which was known as 'Euclid' well into the nineteenth century.

Page 18: *Hauke Haien – as the boy was called.* 'Hauke' is the Friesian form of the old German name 'Hugo'. Commonly used in East Friesland, west of the Elbe along the Lower Saxon coast. It was not until the influ-ence of Storm's Novelle that it began to be used in North Friesland.

Page 18: *barrowing earth during the Easter to November season.* Spring was the time for repairing the winter's damage to the dykes, and autumn the time for preparing and securing their surface against the forthcoming winter storms. The wheelbarrow was first introduced into North Fries-land in 1610 by the Dutch *Deichbauingenieur* Johann Claussen Roll-wagen. In conjunction with the tip-cart (see note to page 77), this addi-tional and efficient means of transporting the considerable amounts of clay, earth or sand needed, particularly to the higher levels of a dyke, marked the beginning of a new era in dyke repair and building.

Page 19: *the turbulent waves ... beat ... against the turf of the dyke.* To protect a dyke constructed of clay and sand against surface run-off, and in more exposed sea-facing positions against wave attack, its surface is covered by short grass or turf, maintained short by sheep grazing (the hooves of heavier animals would damage the surface of the dyke).

Page 20: *wonder-boy from Lübeck.* Christian H. Heineken of the Baltic city of Lübeck, born on 6 February 1721. He was taught universal history at the age of fifteen months and by the end of his third year was well versed in Danish history. He died in his fifth year.

Page 20: *The seaward side is too steep.* North Friesian dykes of the period had varying profiles, from the steep-fronted 'palisade dykes' (*Stackdeiche*), first recorded in the region in the latter half of the sixteenth century, to the smooth-sloped dykes introduced by Dutch engineers in the early seventeenth century. Storm's story creates the impression that all dykes of the mid-eighteenth century were steeply, or abruptly, sloped on their seaward sides, which was not in fact so. Generally speaking, flattening the slope of a dyke reduces the wave pressure on it and lessens foreshore erosion.

Page 20: *if the same thing happens again as it has more than once in the past.* Reference to earlier severe storms that struck the coast of North Friesland, the most notable being in 1362, 1436, 1532, 1570, 1634, 1655 and 1717. The great storm of October 1634 drowned over 6000 people and 50,000 head of cattle, destroyed some 1300 homes and completely changed the coastline of North Friesland. Memories of such storms were passed down from generation to generation. 'The North Sea is a murderous sea,' is an old saying of the region, 'and where there was once water, it can swiftly return again.'

Page 20: *the walk northwards towards the sea.* The local coastline before the great storm of 1634 included a Bredstedt Bay (Bredsteder Werck) which lay to the north of the Hattstedt marsh, the setting of the story. Directly westwards lay the island of Old Nordstrand, the 'other side' or 'other shore'. In the 'pre-1634' topography of the story Hauke could walk northwards from his father's house towards the then Bredstedt Bay to reach the sea (see maps on pages 10 and 11). Today the sea lies directly to the west of the Hattstedt marsh.

Page 20: *All Saints' Day ... a time ... generally not welcomed in Friesland.* A religious festival celebrated on 1 November and which occurs during a period noted in North Friesian chronicles as a time of the worst storms. Autumn storms are particularly severe when occurring with spring, or flood, tides.

Page 20: *a spring tide.* A tide with a range higher than ordinary tides, occurring twice monthly when the moon, sun and earth are in alignment, so that gravitational effects are reinforced.

Page 21: *corpses were discovered washed up on the shore.* Not uncommon in coastal regions such as North Friesland. Tidal flats are dangerous places, particularly during incoming tides that trap the unwary. In a letter to his son Hans dated 5 May 1868, Storm recounts how four years earlier, as *Landvogt* in Husum, a post that combined the duties of Judge and Chief Constable, he had suddenly been called away from home to investigate a gruesome corpse that had been washed up on the shore.

Page 21: *more like sea-devils!* Refers to the corpse's likeness to a large marine fish with spiky head and large mouth (*Lophius piscatorius*).

Page 23: *He had been confirmed for well over a year.* Confirmation was traditionally the 'school-leaving examination' and normally took place on some notable date in the religious calendar. It served not only to examine children's reading and writing abilities and religious knowledge, but also marked a new phase in their lives. Hauke's ability to read and write at the time of his confirmation was not particularly common among marsh farmers' children, who frequently reached the age of confirmation without being able to do so, the demands of the marshland taking precedence over the need for regular schooling.

Page 23: *his voyage to Spain.* By the middle of the eighteenth century the number of North Friesian seamen was reputed to have been around three thousand, many of whom were employed aboard whalers bound for Greenland; others were employed aboard ships carrying livestock, dairy or cereal produce to other parts of the world.

Page 23: *a small thatched cottage ... on the dyke.* Small cottages of the type occupied by Trin' Jans were generally the home of a smallholder or a day-labourer. In earlier times, as a protection against high water, such cottages were built either on the dykes themselves or on their landward sides. The last cottage of this kind – a cottage built on a sea dyke on the island of Nordstrand – was destroyed in the storm of 1936.

Page 24: *the uplands above the marsh.* The 'Geest'. The extensive, partly cultivated, higher moraine land of Schleswig-Holstein stretching from Flensburg in the north to the river Elbe in the south.

Page 24: *a kingfisher.* Superstitiously held to be a lucky bird; also called 'halcyon' after the Greek legend of the faithful lover Halcyon. Its feathers were sometimes sewn into a person's clothing to protect both life and health. It was also believed to have the ability to calm stormy weather. To kill such a bird could only bring misfortune to the slayer.

Page 25: *shrimp fishing.* Mainly the occupation of women who, in the late summer at ebb tide, manually 'trawled' for shrimps along the floor of the mudflats. A wooden- or metal-framed shrimping net affixed to a pole, known locally as a *Gliep*, would be firmly pushed along the muddy floor of the flats by the fisherwoman while she waded waist-deep in the receding waters. She would lift the net clear of the water from time to time to empty it of its catch, which she would tip into a large bag hung round her waist.

Page 26: *Christian the Fourth crown piece.* Christian IV, popular King of

Denmark, 1588-1648. Both the duchies of Schleswig and Holstein, including North Friesland, were held in union with Denmark from 1460 to 1864. The coin, the *Krone*, was of silver, seldom gold, and embossed with a crown.

Page 27: *the knacker in the town*. The knacker, or horse-slaughterer, customarily lived outside the walls of the town, mainly because of the offensive smells associated with his work.

Page 28: *his father and grandfather were dykemasters before him*. The records of dykemasters in the Hattstedt marsh since 1634 show that prominent farming families in the district were providers of successive dykemasters; most notably the family of Iwersen-Schmidt of Lunden-berg, which between 1812 and 1921 provided four dykemasters. It has been suggested that a contemporary and friend, Johann Iwersen-Schmidt (1798-1875), was a model for Storm's dykemaster. He was owner of the Lundenberg farmstead and dykemaster in the Hattstedt marsh from 1837 until 1875. A necessary requirement for the post was substantial land-ownership; hence Hauke's father's mocking remark about the ownership of 'twenty-nine fens'.

Page 28: *Martinmas*. The feast of St Martin on 11 November, normally celebrated with the eating of a goose, the Martinmas goose. In country life the feast marked the end of the harvest, and in the marshland the time when the annual dyke and sluice accounts detailing the year's main-tenance costs were generally prepared. Sluices were built into the dykes to carry away the water from the polders or lowlands, the rates of flow being controlled by means of sluicegates.

Page 29: *the tallest tree in the village, a mighty ash*. The ash is the most common species of tree found in the North Friesian marshlands and was frequently planted among the farmsteads. It has a long association with superstition, from the curing of infirm children to protection against storms and witchcraft. In Germanic mythology it has a special place as the 'world tree', Yggdrasil, whose branches reached out across the whole world. In Storm's Novelle the ash is associated with key events in the lives of the central characters.

Page 30: *the dykemaster's spacious living room*. The interior decoration of old-style North Friesian farmhouses reflected the taste of the eight-eenth century, with its strong West Friesian and Dutch influences. Dec-oration of walls with Dutch tiles and wooden panelling, and the use of alcove, or recessed, box-beds also served the purpose of conserving heat. The adjoining guests' room, the *Pesel*, often known as the 'best room' in the house, was also used as a storage room, and was used as a living and dining room only on the occasion of a family festival or funeral.

Page 32: *that fat Niss.* The mischievous household sprite Niss Puk, or Nisskuk, a popular figure among the legends of Schleswig-Holstein, was often said to be seen sitting up in the haylofts of farmhouses. Groats and butter were frequently left out for him at night. If well-treated he would bring good fortune to the farm and its animals, but if offended, could bring disaster.

Page 33: *Squire, ... that is what people call their employer in these parts.* The form of address here is in Low German (*Uns' Weert*). *Herr* (sir) is used later in the text as an alternative form of address. Storm's use of Low German (Plattdeutsch) here and elsewhere in the Novelle gives it a precise regional tone for the period.

Page 34: *the member of the dyke committee who is responsible.* Up to the beginning of the nineteenth century the length of a dyke was divided for administrative purposes between the local communities it was built to protect. In the Hattstedt marsh region in the eighteenth century the dyke was divided into ten parts, each known as an *Edigelag*. The responsibility and costs for the maintenance of each part were apportioned among the associated community's landowners, who might also be dyke committee members.

Page 35: *the weather will drive its way into the dyke there!* Deep penetration of water into a hole or fissure in the seaward side of a dyke can cause a shallow slump in its landward side which ultimately leads to breaching. The rules and regulations governing dyke maintenance and use have always been extremely strict, their flouting punished by fines imposed by a local court. The surface of the dyke was of particular importance; upon its condition depended the overall safety of the dyke itself, and damage to it had to be repaired in the shortest possible time. The poor condition and abuse of the dyke as described by Hauke would have had significant meaning to readers who lived under the protection of dykes and in constant fear of a breach. The description paints a picture of a seriously lax, and ultimately disastrous, dyke administration.

Page 35: *straw laying and fixing.* A maintenance process known locally as *Bestickarbeiten* or *Bestickungsarbeiten*. Rye or wheat straw was used to protect the toe (leading seaward edge) of the dyke against ice and winter storms; reed was also used given its ready availability in the marshlands. The straw was laid on the dyke to cover it from its toe to slightly above the high-water line, then secured to the dyke by straw-rope. The rope was first stretched over the laid straw, then at regular intervals pushed several inches, staple-like, into the clay by means of a two-pronged fork, a *Sticknagel*. The finished covering had the appearance of carefully woven, thick matting, which was also used to protect damaged areas of dyke exposed to the sea. The 'straw laying and fixing' had to be completed by the autumn. In the spring, after the winter weather, the 'matting' would normally need to be re-secured to the dyke.

Page 36: *doesn't have enough clay under his feet.* A local expression, meaning that Hauke does not own enough land to be appointed dyke-master.

Page 36: *those few acres of his father's.* The old unit of area used in the North Friesian marshes was the *Demat*, also known as a *Tagesmahd*: the area (grass or cornland) which a man could mow with a scythe in one day. The measure was equal to about 1.5 acres, but there were regional variations.

Page 36: *the district's Amtmann and chief dykemaster.* In addition to dyke administration, the chief dykemaster's duties as Amtmann also included supervision of the district's judicial and administrative affairs, and within the duchies of Schleswig and Holstein power was vested in him to do this. Such administrative affairs included the maintenance of roads and transport and the levying of dues and taxes.

Page 38: *"Eisboseln".* A traditional North Friesian winter sport that has long been part of local culture. Originating in Holland, where it was played as early as the fourteenth and fifteenth centuries, it is first record-ed in North Friesland in 1757. A village team would first challenge another by sending it a *Bosselkugel*, the lead-filled wooden ball used in the contest. The teams would meet, and whichever team's ball struck a distant object first won the match. The game remains extremely compet-itive to this day, with players and spectators shouting: *Lüch op un fleu herut!* ('Soar and fly far!') at a particular throw. The ball is of varying size and can weigh up to one pound; it can be thrown considerable dis-tances. The technique for throwing it is similar to that used for throwing a discus.

Page 38: *the broad, stone church tower.* The descriptions throughout the Novelle of this church and its surroundings strongly suggest that Storm had in mind the thirteenth-century St Marienkirche in the village of Hattstedt, four miles north of Husum. The tower and spire, thought to have been built in 1639, are together a distinctive feature of the flat local landscape, towering above the marshlands and dykes. The tower is built of large, square stone blocks. Storm married his second wife, Dorothea Jensen, in the old parsonage near to the St Marienkirche on 13 June 1866. The church is the spiritual centre of the North Friesland parish that today encompasses the villages of Wobbenbüll, Hattstedter Marsch, Horstedt and Hattstedt.

Page 41: *That was a fine throw, said Zacharias* ... A customary expression associated with the contest.

Page 42: *the Archangel Michael himself.* The guardian angel of Israel, who in the Book of Revelation leads the hosts of heaven to battle against Satan. In paintings he is depicted with a flaming sword and sometimes a pair of scales. His feast day, Michaelmas, is on 29 September.

Page 43: *ten feet.* The *Fuss* (foot), which originally measured 11.8 inches, had been used in North Friesland since at least the sixteenth century. There were many regional variations, with over one hundred different lengths ranging from 9.8 to 13.4 inches being recorded. In Schleswig-Holstein the unit in general use was the *Hamburger Fuss* measuring 11.25 inches. Other early units of length in North Friesland with similar regional variations were the *Ellen* (ca two feet) and the *Ruthe* (ca five yards).

Page 45: *the "guildroom".* A large room in a village inn used by local guilds, or societies, for meetings.

Page 45: *a two-step.* A quick, whirling dance in two-four time in which the partners held each other's shoulders.

Page 46: *the town.* I.e. Husum (see note to page 14).

Page 49: *she's dying too: the sickness of these parts, cancer.* Storm was to die of stomach cancer himself on 4 July 1888, five months after completing his Novelle. 'Don't let that frightful word shock you,' he wrote to his son Karl on 10 May 1887, after the cause of his illness had been diagnosed; 'many suffer from it for years and end up dying of something else. The good news is, there's strength enough for me to work in the mornings. I hope it will remain so.'

Page 50: *Westerkoog.* 'West polder'. Polders on the west coast of Schleswig-Holstein were frequently denoted by points of the compass, but there is no firm evidence to suggest that Storm here has an existing polder in mind.

Page 51: *where the Hauke Haien Polder begins.* Believed to refer to the Hattstedt New Polder, 1512 ('Nie koog' or Hattstedter Neuer Koog) in the Hattstedt marsh prior to the great storm of 1634 (see map on page 10). It should not be confused with the polder eventually named after Hauke Haien, the Hauke-Haien-Koog, which today lies further north along the coast opposite the island of Föhr. The new polder, formally opened in 1961 in honour of Storm's Novelle and as a symbol of all dykemasters in the land, has no connection with the polder in the story.

Page 54: *In the uplands, on the western side of the cemetery that sur-*

rounded the church, was a well-kept family grave. In the western part of the cemetery that surrounds the St Marienkirche in Hattstedt lies the grave of the former dykemaster Johann Iwersen-Schmidt as well as those of other members of this influential dykemaster family (see note to page 28). As a friend of the family, it is most likely that Storm attended his funeral and that many details of it found their way into the description of the funeral and burial of Tede Volkerts.

Page 54: *THIS IS DEATH ... JUDGMENT DAY.* This text and that of the epigram on page 55 are in Low German (Plattdeutsch).

Page 54: *Volkert Tedsen ... Tede Volkerts.* Adherence to hereditary family names was common among the Friesians well into the eighteenth century. The son received his own Christian name, but his surname was derived from his father's Christian name, the added -s, -en, -n, -sen or -son signifying the genitive. Tede Volkerts' Christian name was the Christian name of his grandfather following the choice of his parents:

Grandfather:	Tede
Father:	Volkert Tedsen
Son:	Tede Volkerts

Page 55: *a bottle of Langkork.* A bottle of superior wine with a long cork.

Page 55: *the brass knobs on the heating stove.* Heating of rooms in Friesian houses was normally provided by a large iron stove (*Beilegerofen*) ornamented with brass knobs at its corners. It was often richly decorated on three of its sides with scenes from the Bible. Its fourth side was affixed to an adjoining kitchen wall, through which it derived its heat from an adjacent kitchen hearth. Its two supporting legs were made of iron or wood and its thin top plate provided means for keeping food warm. This form of heating had been in use in Friesland since the seventeenth century.

Page 55: *nothing now glinted in the room.* Referring to the practice of covering reflecting surfaces during a funeral meal to avoid anything gleaming or glittering. According to ancient custom, whoever saw his or her reflection in a house in which a person had died must also die.

Page 56: *a riding tournament.* The *Ringreiten*, an equestrian event in which a competitor with a lance rode at a slow gallop while trying to pierce a freely suspended small metal ring. The rings varied in size down to the 'King's Ring' which had the smallest diameter. The winner, or 'king', was the competitor who pierced the most rings during the competition. The sport has been played in the Hattstedt marsh for many centuries and is still popular there today.

Page 56: *the white clay pipes were fetched from the corner.* White pipes with long stems, introduced into North Friesland from Holland around 1700. A pipe-rack was a normal feature of most Friesian living rooms.

Page 61: *the main dyke.* The sea dyke, a dyke that directly fronts the North Sea, distinct from a secondary, or inland, dyke built in former times to protect earlier polders from the sea, but now found situated inland owing to later land reclamation occurring in front of it. Many inland dykes, sometimes known as `sleeping dykes', exist across the country today, some serving as a second line of defence.

Page 61: *the wide expanse of foreland.* Land accumulated through decades of sea action; here the land lying on the seaward side of the dyke. Not to be confused with the 'foreshore', a term loosely applied to that part of the seashore lying between the lowest low-water line and the average high-water line.

Page 62: *a polder of about fifteen hundred acres.* Believed to refer to the Hattstedt New Polder ('Nie koog' or Hattstedter Neuer Koog, 1512) shown by the Husum cartographer Johannes Mejer in Danckwerth's *Landesbeschreibung* (1652). The general area and outline of the Hattstedt New Polder are similar to those described by Storm (see map on page 10).

Page 63: *they said that a gypsy's baby was thrown into it.* The source of this story is to be found in a folktale collection, to which Storm contributed, edited by Karl Müllenhof (1818-84), *Sagen, Märchen und Lieder der Herzogtümer Schleswig, Holstein und Lauenburg* (Kiel, 1845), in a story about a breach in a dyke that could not be filled. The workmen asked the advice of a wise old woman who told them that the breach could be filled only if a living child were to be buried voluntarily in it. A gypsy woman passed by with a child, and was offered a thousand crowns for it which she readily accepted. Bread was then placed at the end of a long plank and pushed out so that it overhung the middle of the breach. The hungry child, seeing the bread, crawled out along the plank to get it, and reaching the middle of the breach, was hurled down into its depths when the workmen pulled the plank away. The breach in the dyke was soon filled with earth and the danger averted. It is said that a hollow can be seen in that place to this day and is always covered by sea grass.

Page 66: *a small hallig which people called "Jeverssand", also "Jevers-hallig".* Early maps of the Hattstedt marsh coastal region show that a *hallig*, or small island, named Harmelfshallig or Jacobshallig, existed in the then Bredstedt Bay (Bredstedter Werck) before the great storm of 1634. Storm used such early maps himself in his own researches, and it

131

is likely that the "Jevershallig" here described and the hallig shown on earlier maps were one and the same.

Page 67: *peat circles*. Peat was often stacked in circular piles to dry.

Page 68: *I've attached some nails to the cord*. A possible reference to the superstitious belief that iron deters evil. Metallic substances were often believed to counteract the influence of witchcraft and every kind of evil spirit.

Page 72: *the Damm behind the harbour.* A road of that name leads south out of the town of Husum today.

Page 72: *looked in the horse's mouth*. The usual method of determining a horse's age, by the examination of its teeth.

Page 72: *Slovak*. A term used to denote a gypsy. Gypsies at the time were known in Germany as wily horse-dealers who were frequent visitors to cattle-markets and horse-fairs.

Page 76: *it will make the Lawrence Boy look like a midget*. The son of Laurentius Damm, a citizen of Hamburg who lived in the late sixteenth century, was said to measure about nine feet in height at his confirmation.

Page 77: *if we have ... clay on the seaward side, on the landward side or in the middle we can mostly use sand!* Present-day dykes are similarly constructed, with the bulk of the construction being of sand, clay being used only on their seaward sides as a direct defence against wave attack. Earlier, smaller dykes were constructed mostly of earth and clay, but as they continued to grow in size the amounts of clay needed became prohibitive. The clay (*Kleierde*), a mixture of mud and sand, which was used was normally taken from the immediate foreland. Present-day dykes are significantly wider and higher than they were in the seventeenth and eighteenth centuries.

Page 77: *horse-drawn tip-carts with shafts*. Small, two-wheeled wagons that could readily be unhitched from the horses and their loads of clay tipped onto the dyke. They were used extensively where large amounts of clay or sand had to be transported over long distances and at the lower levels of dyke construction; the higher levels were too steep for the horses and there the wheelbarrow was used (see note to page 18).

Page 82: *The dyke now rose nearly eight feet above the level of the polder.* Just over half the dyke's intended height of some fifteen feet. The building of a dyke to roughly half its height, leaving it open to the sea for the winter and completing it the following spring, was the practice of the leading dyke-builder of the day, Jean Henri Desmercieres (1687-1778). His dykes, reflecting earlier Dutch designs, were sloped on their seaward sides and were around sixteen feet in height. He was responsible for the creation of three polders in the region, one of which, north of Husum, carries his name to this day; the other two were named after princesses of the ruling houses (see note to page 91).

Page 82: *childbed fever.* Puerperal fever. A serious, formerly widespread form of blood-poisoning caused by infection contracted during child-birth. Storm's wife Constanze died from puerperal fever in 1865.

Page 83: *warming pan.* An early form of hot water bottle: long-handled brass pan in which either hot coals or stones were placed.

Page 83: *the conventicle meetings held by that Dutch tailor.* Secret religious assemblies, especially of Nonconformists or Dissenters. Dutchmen were generally at the forefront of such movements in North Friesland in both the seventeenth and eighteenth centuries which witnessed the spread of such groups as the Mennonites.

Page 83: *The separatist conventicle movement.* The Pietist movement: originally a movement within Lutheranism in the seventeenth century that emphasised spiritual and devotional faith rather than theology and dogma. It strongly influenced other groups, such as the Moravians, Methodists and Evangelicals, and spread from Holland to North Fries-land where it gained a strong footing. The members within a communi-ty elected their own pastor and drew up a church covenant, or compact, which all signed. The established Churches regarded the Pietists as radi-cals.

Page 86: *it rose about fifteen feet above normal tide-level.* See note to page 82.

Page 87: *the steep walls of the dyke; the void between them had now to be filled.* The closing of a tideway, or watercourse, was a most danger-ous and risky operation. The swift-flowing mass of water developed enormous force when restricted, and could often rip away large sections of the dyke walls before being finally stopped.

Page 88: *if your dyke's going to hold, something live's got to go into it!* An expression of the superstitious belief of the region that only the bury-ing of a living thing within a breach or gap in a dyke could ensure its per-manent closure and thus the safety of the dyke (see note to page 63).

Page 89: *What catechism did you learn that from?* In the Protestant regions of Germany Luther's so-called *Kleine Katechismus* (1529) remains the foundation for religious instruction in church and school.

Page 90: *thousand-voiced chorus of honking brent geese.* The North Sea Tidal Flats are still a feeding and resting place for Arctic geese, especially the brent and the barnacle, on their way to their breeding or winter quarters. They gather in tens of thousands on the foreshores and the Halligen.

Page 90: *the Royal Government Commissioners.* Officials appointed by the current administration with special responsibilities; here the assessment of the new dyke. Taxes arising from reclaimed land were an important source of income for the authorities and provided much of the impetus for land reclamation.

Page 91: *the "New Caroline Polder".* It was customary to name a new polder (*Koog*) after a princess of a ruling house, e.g. the Margarethen Koog (1511), the Elizabeth Sophien Koog (1739) and the Juliane Marien Koog (1777-8) which can be found on maps today. Although the 'New Caroline Polder' is imaginary, Storm is believed to have had in mind the Hattstedt New Polder, the Hattstedter Neue Koog (1512), which lies just north of Husum. Its shape and location closely match his descriptions.

Page 91: *spread the clay from the ditches.* The clearing and spreading of the mounds of clay that were left after the maintenance of the drainage ditches in the polder. Work that was normally done in the winter when the clay had dried out and was brittle.

Page 91: *the hitherto nominal shares in the polder.* In proportion to the number of shares held in the foreland, the landowners first received 'ideal' or nominal shares in the new polder until such time as its real value, that is, the overall productivity of the land, could be assessed; usually some three to four years after the initial dyking. The nominal shares were then converted into actual shares, or plots, in the reclaimed land. The new polder was unfit for profitable use until the high salt levels in the ground had been reduced through rainfalls, a process taking some four to five years.

Page 92: *sugar chests.* Originally made for the importing of raw sugar into Europe. They were of hard, tropical-American wood and often used for storage or to make items of household furniture.

Page 97: *Trin' Jans was telling her a story.* Storm's model for Trin' Jans was Lena Wies (1797-1869), the storyteller of his youth, who furnished him with material for his Novellen. From her he had learned the craft of storytelling and the legends, ghost stories and fairy tales of his homeland. She lived in Husum, where her family ran a bakery. In his youth Storm had been more deeply influenced by her than by anyone else. In his sketch *Lena Wies* (1873) he erected a literary monument to this Scheherazade of his boyhood: 'What a storyteller she was! – in Plattdeutsch, in low tones, with devout solemnity ... everything in her mouth acquired its original stamp and rose up as large as life before her hearers as though from some mysterious depth.'

Page 98: *"Child," said the old woman, "it was a mermaid; they are monsters who cannot be blessed."* The old woman's story has close similarities with the legendary tale of the 'sea-woman of Haarlem' who, swimming in the Zuider Zee during a great storm on the coasts of Holland and Friesland, was swept into a polder through a breach in a dyke in the Purmermer. She became stranded when the storm abated and the breach was repaired. The strange creature was said to have become accustomed to the land and the people and to have lived in Haarlem for fifteen years, and to have been buried in a churchyard on account of the reverence she had always paid to the cross. One of the characteristics of mermaids is their lack of a soul.

Page 100: *marsh fever*. Malaria.

Page 100: *a maze of mouse-holes*. Mouse- and mole-holes are particularly dangerous to a dyke, causing seepage of water into its main body. Subsequent hydrostatic pressures transmitted via wave action in an underlying layer can considerably reduce the stability of the dyke, often leading to a breach.

Page 101: *brushwood groynes*. Fences on the tidal flats that prevented mud drift along the shores. They consisted of two rows of posts spaced 10 to 12 inches apart, usually 2 to 2½ feet in height, between which brushwood and branches of fir were laid.

Page 101: *a tide as in 1655*. The great storm of 4 August 1655 when the dyke was breached from Bredstedt to Husum. The details of this storm are recorded in Antonius Heimreich's *Nordfresische Chronick* (1668), a source frequently used by Storm for his Novelle.

Page 104: *storm ... finally veered to the north-west*. Storms from the north-west in the autumn are especially feared in North Friesland.

Page 105: *the year 1756, which will never be forgotten in these parts.* The storm that struck North Friesland on 7 October 1756. 'The 11th of September in the year 1751 was a day to remember, but the 7th of October of the year 1756 will stay in the minds of many more as the more terrible and frightening ... The fury of the storm was indescribable. It appeared as if the towering roaring waves wanted to sweep every house away at once ... They breached the Hattstedt marsh dyke and a breach pond was formed of some 7 Ruhten wide and 16 Ruhten deep' (Johann Lass, *Sammlung einiger Husumischer Nachrichten,* Flensburg, 1750 ff.). (One Ruhte [Ruthe] = ca five yards.)

Page 105: *"Help me! Help me! ... God have mercy on the others!"* One of the passages in the Novelle where Storm's use of Low German (Plattdeutsch) achieves an elemental grandeur (see also notes to pages 15, 33, 54 and 97).

Page 106: *the golden cockerel on the church spire had been brought down by a whirlwind.* The spire of the St Marienkirche, Hattstedt was struck and set on fire during a storm in 1751, and further struck during Storm's lifetime in 1827, 1859 and 1878.

Page 106: *huge swarms of flies and other troublesome insects descended from the sky like snow.* Signs of this kind have frequently been chronicled as foretelling catastrophes. Those described here closely match those contained in Antonius Heimreich's *Nordfresische Chronick.*

Page 106: *at the corner by the pharmacy.* The Unicorn pharmacy (Einhorn-Apotheke) that once stood at the corner of the market-place in Husum. It remains identified today by the figure of a white unicorn over a shop-front. On market days it was a place where women from the country stood to sell butter and eggs.

Page 108: *The wind's veered! ... – to the north-west, on a half spring-tide!* The description here of wind behaviour and tidal condition, and the earlier indication of the time of night, eight o'clock, closely follow the chronicled accounts of great storms that struck North Friesland in 1634, 1717 and 1756. The chronicle of 1634 reads: 'In the year 1634, towards evening on the day before All Saints [...], a great storm came in from the sea, from the south-west. It was about seven or eight in the evening. [...] The waves were hitting the dyke, then rising up and falling onto the roof of the house. [...] Then the wind began to come from the west with such fury that no sleep came to our eyes [...], the water was as high as the dyke ridge [...]. The wind veered slightly to the north-west and thundered against the farmstead with such force as I have never experienced in my life before' (M. Lensch, *Jan Adriaans Leeghwater und seine Beschreibung der grossen Sturmflut vom 11. Oktober 1634).*

Page 114: *The storm had seized his cape, it would soon have torn him from his horse.* Hans Iwert Schmidt, dykemaster in the Hattstedt marsh from 1812, was killed in a storm in 1814 when the wind caught his cape, suddenly lifting it up over his head; his horse shied, tossing him into a ditch in which he drowned.

Page 116: *they gave Socrates poison to drink.* At the age of seventy, the Athenian philosopher was convicted of 'impious' teaching and sentenced to death by drinking hemlock.

Page 116: *that we can do every day.* When Storm corrected proofs for the first magazine publication in February/March 1888 he cut a passage of several paragraphs following these words. It contained a detailed eye-witness account of the dykemaster's death-plunge from his former farm-hand Carsten who claimed to have seen him held in mid-air in the claws of a demonic apparition, and further reflections on the dykemaster's phantomisation from the schoolmaster who went on to offer a rational explanation for the second narrator's encounter. Faced with this passage in proof, Storm found it, as he told his publishers, 'too out of keeping with the prevailing tone'.

Page 116: *The windows here were above the ridge of the dyke.* See note to page 15.

Page 116: *he belongs to the rationalists!* Storm uses the word *Aufklärer* – philosopher, or adherent, of the Enlightenment, the eighteenth-century European intellectual movement that stressed the primacy of reason and scientific knowledge and the need for critical reappraisal of existing social institutions. The movement was generally hostile to religion.

Afterword

by David A. Jackson

Until recently Theodor Storm was widely seen as a regional writer whose Novellen revolved round his home town and his family's patrician past; by and large, it was claimed, he was uninterested in political issues and ignorant of the great ideological debates of his time. The hallmark of his Novellen was allegedly the evocation of *Stimmung,* mood: wistful nostalgia pervaded a fictional world governed by transience, renunciation and death. This view did scant justice to Storm's achievement.[1]

His life was anything but a provincial idyll.[2] Born in 1817 in Husum, a small coastal town in the then Danish duchy of Schleswig, Storm as a child felt starved of affection by emotionally undemonstrative parents. His sense of individual isolation bred a longing for love and security which became a leitmotif in his works. While studying law in Kiel (and briefly in Berlin) from 1838 to 1842, he joined a circle of students round the Mommsen brothers, Tycho and Theodor. The latter was to achieve renown as a historian of Ancient Rome, and a promoter of the study of history as a means of raising popular political consciousness. Through this circle Storm encountered the works of contemporary German writers and philosophers like the humanitarian atheist, Ludwig Feuerbach. With the Mommsens he published a joint collection of poems in 1843, his own contributions being largely love poems.

He returned to Husum and set up practice there. There was no demand for his poetry, but a Schleswig-Holstein annual commissioned lighter, humorous pieces from him to offset learned contributions on evangelical, economic and German-national issues. The constraints, however, were undeniable. Non-anodyne love poetry and atheistic pieces were taboo. Storm had to cloak his humanitarian message. In 1846 he married his cousin, Constanze

Esmarch, in a non-church marriage, and later insisted that no pastor should officiate at either his or his wife's funeral. Soon after his marriage, however, he fell passionately in love with Dorothea Jensen, the daughter of a Husum senator, and set up a *ménage à trois*. When Dorothea left Husum, his anguish was deep and permanent. His story *Immensee* (1849) indirectly captured much of his self-reproach at lacking the courage to confront society's conventions.

In 1848 he was involved in the rising against the Danes that was part of the revolutionary tide sweeping continental Europe in that year. He hoped for a united, democratic German republic and for a time provided local reports for the newspaper of the Provisional Government. After the restored Danish authorities had refused to confirm his licence to practise, he was accepted into the Prussian judiciary and left Husum for Potsdam in 1853. Storm still regarded himself primarily as a love poet who would develop the German tradition in the direction of a Feuerbachian affirmation of sex and passion. But the market for such poetry, especially if it challenged conventional moral notions, shrank drastically after 1848 in the climate of harsh repression. The public clamoured for prose. *Immensee* had become a bestseller among well-to-do ladies in Berlin. But it was mistakenly read as affirming the sanctity of marriage in the face of adulterous temptations; its critical stance went unheeded. Henceforth Storm was labelled an exquisite purveyor of wistfulness and a creator of *Stimmung*.

In 1856 Storm was appointed to the County Court in Heiligenstadt, a town in the staunchly Catholic Eichsfeld area. His experiences here refuelled his pre-revolutionary hatred of the aristocracy and his rejection of Christianity and the church. In the early 1860s he committed himself to the democratic cause and the championing of humanitarian values, writing for the mass-circulation periodical *Die Gartenlaube (The Arbour)*. Liberal-democratic hopes were high, and Bismarck's assumption of the Prussian chancellorship in 1862 initially seemed the last despairing throw of moribund Junkerism. When the German population in Schleswig and Holstein rose against the Danes in 1863/4, Storm was democratically elected *in absentia* as Husum's *Landvogt*, a post combining policing and judicial duties.

But hopes of an independent, democratic Schleswig-Holstein

soon evaporated. First, Austria and Prussia jointly ruled the duchies; then, after the Austro-Prussian War, Prussia annexed both duchies in 1867. Bitterly disillusioned by these developments and by the capitulation of Prussian liberals once Bismarck's policies promised to bring German unification a stage nearer, Storm accepted the post of *Amtsrichter*, a judge in the lowest court, rather than risk being involved in political measures. He did not share the nationalist euphoria of 1870/71 after the defeat of France and the founding of the German Empire. With the demise of democratic republicanism and the denunciation of enlightened, cosmopolitan principles, Storm became increasingly isolated ideologically.

By 1870 his world had collapsed on all fronts. Constanze had died in 1865, while Dorothea Jensen, whom he married after some hesitation in 1866, could cope neither with a large household of young daughters and difficult teenage sons nor with Storm's cult of his dead wife. She became chronically depressed, and Storm, too, was overtaken by moods of total despair and morbid hypochondria. Even as sixth-formers, his eldest sons, Hans and Ernst, kicked over the traces. At university their riotous living continued, draining Storm's finances. By 1873 it was clear that Hans was an alcoholic. The trials and tribulations of father and son continued until the latter's death in 1886. To compound his problems, his youngest son, Karl, contracted syphilis as a student. In the late 1860s and early 1870s Storm feared that his creative powers had dried up and that his literary career was over.

It was only in the second half of the 1870s that Storm gradually established himself as one of the highest paid contributors to Germany's leading periodicals. The great expansion of the periodical press in the new Empire generated an insatiable need for shorter prose works as publishers and editors fought for subscribers. It was an authors' market, and Storm made full use of this. In fact he had little alternative since his sons devoured his regular earnings. Increasingly frustrated with his judicial duties and aided by his share of his parents' property, he finally retired and built himself a villa in Hademarschen at the end of the 1870s. His trials, however, continued and he was often forced to rush works in order to generate desperately needed cash. After stomach cancer was diagnosed in the spring of 1887, he sank into deep depression and work on his last Novelle, *Der Schimmelreiter*, which he had begun the previous year, was slow. He died five months after finishing it on 4 July 1888.

Attempts to divide Storm's work into neat periods have been unrewarding. The scheme put forward by Franz Stuckert in 1955[3] long held unchallenged sway. Sentimental 'resignation Novellen' mirroring Germany's weak, disunited state in the 1840s and 1850s were seen to predominate in Storm's early career; then in the 1860s modish, superficial 'problem Novellen' akin to the hollow ideals of the liberals and democrats during the Constitutional Struggle in Prussia were supposed to have temporarily flourished; finally, after Bismarck's dynamic policy of blood and iron and the creation of the German Empire in 1871 had revitalised Germany, a reinvigorated Storm was seen as inspired to write tragic 'fate Novellen' in which individuals were pitted either against hereditary problems or, as in *Der Schimmelreiter*, against elemental natural forces and the ignorant masses.

It is altogether more profitable to stress the great continuities observable in Storm's Novellen. From *Marthe und ihre Uhr* (*Marthe and her Clock*, 1847) and *Immensee* (1849) onwards, the theme that constantly recurs is that of individuals moulded by the pressures and expectations of a society dominated by undemocratic ideologies and institutions. Economic backwardness and restricted material and professional circumstances often constitute further obstacles in the path of true happiness. Storm's sympathy in all this is with the individual, not with society, the state or some greater common good. He evolved narrative means of subtly conveying how tragically misguided the actions and motives of his heroes and heroines were, without at the same time alienating and antagonising his publishers, editors or public. Readers had to be manoeuvred into adopting positions at variance with many of their ingrained convictions. Early in his career he experimented with conflicting perspectives. Thus in *Marthe und ihre Uhr* the fictional narrator, with his love of life and his expanded horizons, embodies values far removed from the self-denial practised by the heroine, the victim of a restricting, restricted patriarchal system. In *Immensee* the text itself is constructed so as to invite the reader to criticise the norms promoted and enforced by family and society: it questions the whole middle-class regulation of sex and love to serve considerations of material security and social respectability. Initially Storm employed the artistic technique of focusing on 'lyrical', 'poetic' scenes or situations joined together by the briefest of link-passages, while *Stimmung* or the evocation of mood played a key role in sensitising the reader. But the critical thrust was never drowned by sentiment.

The crushing victory of the counter-revolutionary forces in the German states and Austria after 1848 compelled writers, intellectuals and publicists to reconsider their positions. For many moderate liberals the 'excesses' of the radicals and democrats had been even more traumatic than the violence of the resurgent ruling classes. Hopes of a unified, capitalist Germany, centred on a constitutional Prussian monarchy and enjoying representative institutions based on a restricted franchise, lay in ruins.

Influential publicists and writers like Julian Schmidt and Gustav Freytag set about reconstructing a new literary agenda. They demanded that German writers create a new, distinct form of realism, avoid the critical, radical 'excesses' of the pre-revolutionary period, and concentrate instead on bringing out the underlying beauty, goodness and truth of contemporary socio-economic and political trends.[4] They were not to be guilty of the immoral excesses of French realism – Flaubert was no more esteemed by German opinion than Eugène Sue – nor to dwell on the abuses of middle-class, capitalist society as English realists like the later Dickens did. Nor were they to rely on mystery, melodrama and convoluted plots, i.e. the ingredients that catered for the undemanding readers of the lending libraries. This specifically German Realism was labelled 'true' or 'poetic realism'. The *Wahre*, the true and essential, was to be clearly distinguished from the *Wirkliche*, the merely actual or topical. Only if literature concentrated on evoking 'positive' contemporary trends and the goodness of middle-class life with its sound capitalist ethos, its education, its morality, its order, and so on, could 'realism' be truly poetic. In this context the word 'poetic' was understood, not in the sense of verse, but of true literature or *Dichtung*.

In all this Schmidt and Freytag were adapting to their own conservative liberal, pro-Prussian view of Germany's destiny classical-idealist categories elaborated by Goethe and Schiller. This whole aesthetic scheme rested on a supposed 'identity' or correspondence between form and content. Underlying harmony and beauty whether of the cosmos, contemporary reality, society, or of the integrated individual had to be mirrored by the unity, balance and beauty of the work of art. Epic and drama continued to be thought of as the supreme forms; they would, it was confidently predicted, flourish again in a united Germany. Novelists, in contrast, were looked down upon as the step-brothers of epic poets and even the Novelle with its classical pedigree, its tighter form, its greater unity of content and its use of symbolism would allegedly make way for the 'higher' genres once German unity had been achieved.

Although he shared some of the classical-idealist assumptions underpinning this aesthetic, Storm did not adopt the socio-political emphases of Schmidt or Freytag. At the same time he too was convinced that literature should communicate ideals – in his case humanitarian, democratic ones – and, if only by implication, hold up models to be emulated. Above all, he also subscribed to the Poetic-Realist belief that art had a unique identity. Literature had to mould readers' sensibilities and ideas, not by abstract reasoning or polemic, but by translating ideals and ideas into scenes and sequences envisaged in the round, and in which all the resources of mood, musicality, imagery and symbolism were utilised. These aesthetic principles also reflected – and this has to be stressed – a keen awareness on Storm's part of the demands and sensitivities of the authorities, his publishers and his public. There were certain socio-political, moral and sexual topics that simply had to be cloaked.

In the late 1850s and early 1860s, encouraged by the false spring of the so-called liberal New Era in Prussia, Storm experienced a great creative surge. In works like *Veronica* (1861) or *Im Schloss* (*In the Castle*, 1862), heroines are shown liberating themselves from religious and social prejudices. 'Actual' reality for a while promised to merge with 'true', ideal reality. In contrast, in Novellen like *Auf der Universität* (*At the University*, 1863) or *Drüben am Markt* (*Across the Market Square*, 1863) individuals' attempts to achieve a good life are shown as frustrated by social prejudices and material limitations. Storm's mastery of formal techniques deepened, especially his use of competing perspectives. In general the Novellen of this middle period acquire a more sustained epic texture. The aesthetic goal is a closed, self-contained, balanced work of art in which symbolism plays a key role.

Disappointment in his personal life and disillusionment with Bismarck's Germany prompted Storm to pursue with renewed vigour the theme of individuals struggling towards enlightened, humane positions in a world governed by brutal class domination and rigid orthodoxy. To do this in contemporary settings would have been foolhardy. A member of the Prussian judiciary could not openly express his hatred of Junkerism; nor did he himself want his criticism to be confused with socialist attacks on the imperial German state which in their turn made his middle-class National-Liberal public extremely sensitive to attacks on the *status quo*. He could easily have found himself ostracised by publishers, editors and public alike at a time when he desperately needed additional income. Hence after a brief experiment in the early 1870s with the allusive, satirical, open-ended techniques of Heinrich Heine and E.T.A. Hoffmann, he often turned to the historical Novelle. It gave him scope to exploit to the full the distance between the norms of fictional characters trapped in the mentalities of their time and the ideals suggested by a fictional narrator in an often contemporary framework. A sense of gradual, if frequently painful historical progress could thereby be communicated to the reader. In *Aquis submersus* and *Renate* characters are shown trying to haul themselves out of superstition and fanaticism in a barbaric, feudal world. Tragically, they may sink back into it and condemn their own youthful aspirations. Only rarely did Storm dispense with *Stimmung*. In his view mood was an essential ingredient in the artistic alchemy needed to mould readers' feelings and generate emotional and intellectual energy for particular ideals. The impassive, objective style of Flaubert's *Madame Bovary* was alien to him.

To the material and ideological obstacles in the way of human fulfilment those posed by inherited defects were increasingly added; the hereditary traits of frivolousness and alcoholism wreak havoc, for example, in one of Storm's major Novellen, *Carsten Curator* (1878). Yet while Naturalist elements entered his works, Storm feared that he might be betraying true Poetic Realism by dwelling on what was sordid, ugly and embarrassing. Above all, he feared that he might be denying the principle of hope. To offset this preoccupation with 'sordid' reality, he tended to balance tragic inner stories with optimistic frameworks, to construct idylls, or to engineeer dénouements that were positively operatic. In his last years he experimented with new themes. The results could be challenging, if ultimately unsatisfactory both intellectually and artistically, as in his evocation of the fate of the ex-convict in *Ein Doppelgänger* (1887) or in his treatment of euthanasia in *Ein Bekenntnis* (*A Confession*, 1887). Individually these and other works contain elements that find their way into *Der Schimmelreiter*, but none of them prepares us for the greatness of that final achievement.

The Dykemaster, to use the title of the present English edition, achieves a density of texture unique in Storm's works. It embodies his final humanitarian stance, recapitulating themes and motifs from earlier works, not by straining for symbolic and philosophical profundity but by concentrating on recounting a gripping tale. The Novelle rivets one's interest from the first page to the last with its dynamic tension, its shifting focuses, and its changes of mood and pace.

Storm realised from the outset that a thorough knowledge both of the topography of the coastal area round Husum and of the principles of dyke construction was vital if the story was to make a real impact on the reader's imagination.[5] He liaised closely throughout with a building inspector specialising in the history of dykes, studied maps and books, and consulted chronicles dealing with past floods including that of 1756 which figures in the story. But detail never degenerates into specialist lumber; it is subordinated to strict, artistic purposes. The particulars contribute to the power of the narrative as it relentlessly pushes forward; above all, detail is integrated into an overall pattern of significances which goes far beyond external action. Although the Novelle powerfully evokes the world of the Friesian coast with its customs and characters, real-life towns, villages and locations are not named. The original book edition provided a glossary for inland readers of terms peculiar to North Friesia. If the dialogue strikes one as closer to the levels and rhythms of everyday speech than that in many other Poetic Realist works, it does not emulate the Naturalist attempt to render actual speech; Low German, sparingly used, serves a primarily poetic purpose. The concern for overall artistic effect is greater than that for mimesis.

Storm's main source, a magazine story entitled 'The Ghostly Rider' published in 1838, offered the bare bones of a plot. On the Vistula a narrator has an experience very like that of the magazine narrator in *The Dykemaster*. But there is no suggestion that there may be a plausible rational explanation for the apparition. He is told how a dyke official accused himself of causing a dyke to burst and in despair spurred his horse into the flooded breach. Man and horse reappear whenever danger threatens. It is a short, crude ghost story, totally lacking in what constitutes the essence of Storm's story – the conflict between the third (main) narrator's interpretation and the community's. But it did stimulate Storm's critical and poetic imagination which subterraneously worked on the material over more than four decades.

The complicated narrative framework of *The Dykemaster* is both medium and message. The first narrator, writing in the present, i.e around the 1880s, tells how as a child 'a good fifty years ago' he read a magazine story at his great-grandmother's. The narrator of that story relates events that took place in the 1820s. Finally, the third narrator, the schoolmaster, relates events that took place in the middle of the eighteenth century. Although basing his version of the life of the dykegrave Hauke Haien – the 'dykemaster' of the present edition – on the accounts of those whom he calls reasonable, sensible men and their descendants, he nevertheless also includes material from the very different version current in the community and associated with Antje Vollmers, the present dykemaster's housekeeper.[6]

The schoolmaster narrator is provided with a distinct personal identity which itself is inseparable from his socio-historical one. His whole frame of mind reveals his theological pedigree. He subscribes to a form of Christianity which contains rationalist elements, whereas the rural population in general is orthodox or sectarian – but in either case superstitious. He is the product of an economically static, absolutist society. What, however, makes the story so fascinating and so typical of Storm is that, despite having been shaped by the institutions and ideologies of the *ancien régime*, the schoolmaster is shown groping towards alternative religious, political and social ideas. He tentatively begins to formulate a new vision of individual fulfilment. Like other Storm heroes denied the support of progressive ideologies or socio-economic forces and dependent on their own resources, he cannot, however, resolve contradictions and overcome ambivalent feelings.

The Novelle explores how contemporary issues colour presentation of the past. In this it resembles C.F. Meyer's *Die Hochzeit des Mönchs* (*The Monk's Wedding*, 1884), with which Storm was familiar. There, too, the relation between framework and inner story explores the relationship between writer, narrator and patrons/public; it explores the connection between socio-political and ideological developments in imperial Germany and the structures and mentalities of late medieval, early Renaissance Italy. In Storm's Novelle the schoolmaster's criticism of Hauke's father-in-law and the community around 1750 cloaks his criticism both of the present incompetent, superstitious dykegrave who owes his position to inherited privilege and property and also of the equally unenlightened, pettily selfish village community. But, as in Meyer's Novelle, the historical setting of *The Dykemaster* limits any underlying criticism of contemporary institutions and authorities.

The schoolmaster's attitude to Hauke is ambivalent through and through. A misshapen, frustrated bachelor, he has remained in this community only as a result of an unsuccessful courtship. Presumably he was rejected because he did not have land and property and because his poorly paid job commanded little social esteem. For these reasons he is attracted to Hauke as an *alter ego*. He presents him as a dynamic figure who overcomes all sorts of handicaps to become an innovatory dykegrave enjoying the love and support of his wife, Elke. She stands by him even though he does not have the property to which she could aspire as a dykegrave's daughter.

But the schoolmaster does not present Hauke as a perfect model. Imbued with traditional notions of academic learning, he is suspicious of such an autodidact; himself brought up to know his place in society, he cannot wholeheartedly endorse Hauke's ambition. Any attraction to emergent notions of individual self-

148

fulfilment is balanced by older norms which condemn such behaviour as megalomania and hubris. Confidence in human nature and in the power of human reason to solve practical and theoretical problems plays no part in a system where orthodoxy and sectarianism both reinforce notions of human powerlessness and of the frailty and folly of human works. If the schoolmaster is fascinated by Hauke's refusal to be cowed into submission – behaviour that contrasts with his own inability to do more than voice indirect criticism – this does not preclude guilty feelings of self-reproach for being so resentful and critical of the community's shortcomings. He projects onto Hauke his sense of guilt at such unchristian feelings.

Despite moving in this direction, the schoolmaster does not progress to a purely humanitarian position. Certainly he rejects belief in the devil incarnate, in ghosts and supernatural portents, but he continues to refer to himself as 'an honest Christian soul'; he endorses the view that Hauke's retarded child, Wienke, represents divine punishment; and he cannot decide whether Elke's recovery was due to Hauke's prayer or the doctor's medicine. Above all, despite all the doubts he projects onto Hauke, he cannot break away from the belief in divine providence and a moral world order. If reality is the court of divine justice, he cannot but regard the bursting of the dyke and Hauke's death as the result of divine retribution. He therefore has to build Hauke's death into the scheme of guilt, sin and atonement.

Despite the schoolmaster's emphases, the text itself contrives to depict Hauke as a true humanitarian hero. Storm cleverly engineers a distance between his narrator(s) and the meanings conveyed by the text. Hauke is without ideological support from outside – as a child he simply has a primer and the Bible to read; without a mother's loving guidance; without any initial encouragement from his father who cannot answer his questions, mocks his apparent presumptuousness, and even tries to break his interest in geometry in order to ensure that he follows in his steps as a small farmer. Nevertheless, he prevails because of his natural disposition and inherited talents – and Elke's support. The dyke that he designs and builds profits and protects the whole community.

In intellectual terms he struggles through to positions where his Christian orthodoxy is under severe strain. Thus he questions whether God can work miracles in response to prayers. He also questions the doctrine of divine omnipotence. Whereas the pious see storms and floods as divine visitations and even regard it as sinful to build dykes, he comes to regard his task as being to protect his community against the Lord God's sea. In his words to Wienke out on the dyke as he provides a natural explanation for the apparently ghostly figures, he adopts a form of pantheism. Yet the step he has yet to take is to follow Feuerbach and recognise that there is nothing beyond nature.

The Novelle includes scenes that illustrate the deep psychological appeal of specific Christian doctrines. It echoes many other Storm stories in evoking loneliness and human beings' need to bestow and receive love and affection. Having lost her son, the widow Trin' Jans thus projects her needs onto a tom-cat until more fulfilling, human objects can be found. After her father's death, Elke, too, is shown as needing to believe in a heavenly father and an eternal life. Yet the actual text suggests that of two inscriptions cited, one on the gravestone of Elke's grandfather and one in the family house, the latter, with its humanitarian message, is the truer one: the Novelle does not show 'death [...] devour[ing] us all – wisdom and knowledge'; nor does it exhort human beings to put their trust in an after-life. If the need to believe in providence and a moral world is shown to be especially strong, the end of the story brings out how illusory this confidence is. Those like the villagers who argue that divine punishment overtakes Hauke ignore the fact that Elke and Wienke also perish. What emerges from the Novelle is a godless world where everything depends on human qualities and 'natural' factors.

At the end Hauke may, *in extremis*, relapse into Christian categories and express the hope that his own self-sacrifice can atone for his neglect of his duty and save the community. But the text conveys to the reader that his death has a different significance. Having first assured himself that the village is safe, Hauke plunges into the sea because, without Elke and his child, his life is meaningless. His end is in a sense a love-death. The thrust of the Novelle is to suggest that it is Hauke's works, not his death, that are important.

The Novelle lends no support to the idea either of a ghostly posthumous existence or of an orthodox definition of immortality.

In contrast, it does reiterate Storm's affirmation of human love. In repeated discreet ways, Elke encourages and protects Hauke and intervenes on his behalf. Her love is the cornerstone on which his success depends. She supports and consoles him during all the years of preparation and construction even though his self-sacrificial labours entail loneliness for her and even though she first has to come to terms with apparent childlessness and then with having a mentally retarded child. Hauke's commitment to her is made equally clear. Indeed, the real human climax of the story is the scene where both of them finally admit to themselves and each other that Wienke is mentally retarded. In a society where childlessness or the birth of a physically or mentally handicapped child is attributed to divine displeasure, both parents have grappled in silence with feelings of guilt and anguished ruminations. In this scene the redemptive power of true human communication and mutual support is underlined.

In its evocation of the inadequacies both of the individual and of society in general, the Novelle pays special attention to the role of inherited traits. Hauke's father voices the pessimistic notion that deterioration and degeneration occur in the third generation. Progress and individual achievement will thus always be threatened. If Hauke inherits positive talents from his father, Wienke inherits defective genetic material from her maternal grandfather. Illness, ageing and death also play a marked role, as they must in any serious humanitarian vision of life. Hauke's own 'guilt' is the result of his illness. Strokes, cancer and other forms of death all figure in the story. But what is important is the human response to them. Elke is shown as concerned for her father; Hauke apparently sacrifices his prospects in order to care for his ailing father; later Elke takes in Trin' Jans and cares for her; she in her turn cares for Wienke. Storm's religion of humanity accepts the existence of pain and suffering, but stresses the importance of seeking to remove, minimise or alleviate them by neighbourly love and concern.

If such 'natural', physical factors threaten human endeavour and achievement, so too do the obstacles put in the way of reform-minded, enlightened figures by the rest of society. Ole Peters, Elke's father's senior farmhand and Hauke's bitter rival, who then marries a wealthy farmer's daughter and constantly resists and criticises Hauke's schemes, does not epitomise deeper traditional and communal virtues: he symbolises petty, egoistic ambition and malevolent resentment towards a man who is intellectually his superior and who also puts an end to his ambitions of marrying the dykemaster's daughter. Hauke himself is not some brash, ruthless entrepreneuer intent on his own individual profit: the dyke scheme is a co-operative, communitarian project built around worker participation.[7] As it will benefit everyone, everyone is expected to participate in it in some way. Hauke is shown making every effort to consult the community and involve them at every stage – but to no avail. Democracy at this level is shown not to work. That does not, however, mean that the Novelle commends some *Führer* principle or authoritarian alternative. The withholding of support and co-operation endangers the scheme, breeding undesirable qualities in Hauke and driving him back into the private domain. But in an imperfect world such human impoverishment, alienation and frustration of basic social needs have to be accepted as the price of progress. Whatever tragedy befalls humanity's benefactors, the important thing which should not be obscured – but tragically will be – is that a worthwhile project goes ahead.

The text suggests that Hauke's guilt is not hubris or 'undemocratic' behaviour, but that it lies rather in heeding the advice of the other members of the dyke committee, especially Ole Peters. It is the first and only time he does so against his own better judgement and when he is still weak from illness. In heeding their counsel he betrays and destroys himself and his family; he also betrays and almost destroys the community entrusted to his care. In a godless world good and evil are redefined. Duties are human, social ones, not divine, theological ones. If institutions and offical ideologies do not provide progressive goals and norms, then the small number of individuals who retain some critical independence must try to elaborate their own value systems. Great stress is laid on performing the duties attached to one's office. Injurious actions or acts of omission and negligence become crucial criteria. It is a conception of duty/guilt typical of somebody imbued with Enlightenment, Kantian notions of the moral imperative, and who believed that rational, humane civil servants could strive to promote the universal good. It is this duty that the nineteenth-century dykegrave and his aides neglect in the outer framework. In an ironic anticipation of the graver temptations that will face Hauke and with an equally ironic allusion to the Fall, the second narrator is shown at the beginning telling of how he almost succumbed to the attractions of his relatives' apples. Despite important business, he puts off his departure because of the weather and would have turned back but for knowing that he had already covered more than half the journey. Like the dykegrave at the inn, he clearly likes his comforts and convenience. The implicit suggestion is that few human beings will exhibit the same determination to serve the community as that shown by Hauke.

Storm's experiences had taught him to beware of official heroes and saints. He refused to follow the suggestion of Theodor Mommsen and abandon his minor figures and bourgeois tragedies in favour of heroes on grand historical stages.[8] In commending the achievement of an obscure dykegrave, his Novelle is a democratic work. It prompts the reader to reflect that enlightened, practical small-scale measures for the benefit of one's fellow human beings may be of greater long-term value than the exploits of those lauded by historians and the offical media. But by 1888 Storm had long lost any confidence that reason and truth were values that would universally prevail once outmoded institutions and ideologies had been exposed.

The way in which the second, i.e. the magazine narrator goes about telling his story illustrates how magazine writers and editors consciously neutralise or weaken the thrust of material originally of critical purpose. The schoolmaster himself has no access to the media. In the case of the magazine narrator – a professional writer or at least a contributor to magazines – it is ultimately impossible to tell whether he allies with the schoolmaster but is also conscious of having to satisfy the editors, publishers and readers of the magazine like, for example, the first narrator's senatorial great-grandmother. Such considerations might lead him to highlight the ghost-story element. Alternatively, he may himself be inclined to superstition. The text suggests that fear, cold, tiredness and a primed imagination soon lend ghostly shape to the seagulls brushing past in the uncertain light.

Storm realised that although scholars may lay bare the essence of religion, just as the schoolmaster devotes a lifetime to unmasking the myth surrounding the dykegrave of the previous century, their ideas may be confined to a small circle of educated readers, with no guarantee that they will ever be disseminated to a wider public. In his later years he inclined to the belief that the uneducated classes had an innate capacity for superstition and that this made it easy for the dominant sections of society to promote their ideology and perpetuate human alienation.

The survival and dissemination of humanitarian ideas were as problematic to Storm as was the task of preserving the memory of champions of enlightenment. While Jeremias Gotthelf (1797-1854) and Adalbert Stifter (1805-68) had been preoccupied with how to ensure that future generations preserved the memory of past calamities produced by godless materialism, the problem for Storm was that, given the socio-political interests of the groups controlling the press, schools and universities, champions of enlightenment in past centuries were either ignored and forgotten or their lives and message perverted. But for the facts that the first narrator encountered the story as a child and retold it fifty years later, and the third, the schoolmaster, devoted a lifetime to reconstructing Hauke Haien's life, any critical record of the latter would have been lost.

This question of the transmission of historical knowledge, of the creation of myths and of their socio-political function, had always concerned Storm. What factors operated when historians, theologians and writers compiled their canon of historical figures whose memory was to be preserved? What determined which 'facts' were preserved, which forgotten? Which deeds were highlighted, which played down? And what was the ideological purpose of these presentations? Did not myth and legend often usurp the place of historical fact in order to further specific ideological goals? Storm was heir to a philosophical tradition epitomised by D.F. Strauss, Ludwig Feuerbach and Bruno Bauer, which had sought to lay bare the kernel of historical truth underlying the gospels' accounts of Jesus Christ and to explore the factors generating supernatural myths and legends, and in *The Dykemaster* he enshrined his final thoughts on the subject. On the basis of the scant material afforded by the Vistula legend he worked back from the ghost to the actual historical figure and explored the whole myth-making process. The schoolmaster refers to brutal men of violence and stubborn prelates being turned into saints, and observes that, whereas in earlier centuries the authorities summarily killed off champions of reason and truth like Socrates and Jesus, in modern times they could achieve the same end by turning them into ghosts, i.e. ensuring that the media and opinion-forming institutions distorted and devalued their stance. Storm may not be identical with the schoolmaster, but there is surely a suggestion that Hauke forms a trinity with Socrates and Jesus Christ as a searcher after truth. Both Jesus and Hauke were turned into 'ghosts'. In Jesus's case the Church destroyed the impact of his humanitarian message by transforming a man into a god; in Hauke's case the significance of his life in humanitarian terms was perverted by turning him into a ghost. It is bitterly ironic that he is transformed into a ghost, condemned to make a ghastly, guilt-ridden appearance whenever a dyke is breached, by the very community his labours benefit. The community itself does the establishment's work for it by turning him into a symbol of the sinful folly of purely human endeavour. If the community has an interest in combating enlightenment and *Humanität*, and if superstitions spring eternal in the human breast, how can isolated individuals hope to preserve and disseminate enlightened notions? By the end of his life Storm had few illusions.

Notes

1 M. Mare, *Theodor Storm and his World* (Cambridge, n.d.) was still promoting this view in the 1970s.

2 F. Stuckert, *Theodor Storm. Sein Leben und seine Welt* (Bremen, 1955), with its suspect ideological categories, was for a long time the authoritative biography. P. Goldammer offered a useful corrective in *Theodor Storm. Eine Einführung in Leben und Werk* (Leipzig, 1968), reprinted as the introduction to vol. 1 of his four-volume edition (Aufbau). Recent critical biographies include G. Bollenbeck, *Theodor Storm. Eine Biographie* (Frankfurt, 1988) and my own *Theodor Storm: The Life and Works of a Democratic Humanitarian* (Oxford and New York, 1992), on which the last section of this Afterword is closely based.

3 See Stuckert, op. cit.

4 On German Poetic Realism after 1848 see H. Widhammer, *Realismus und klassizistische Tradition. Zur Theorie der Literatur in Deutschland 1848-1860* (Tübingen, 1972). See also my chapter 'Taboos in Poetic Realism' in *Taboos in German Literature*, ed. D. A. Jackson (Oxford and Providence, RI, 1996), pp. 59-78.

5 K. E. Laage provides detailed information on the genesis and sources of the

work in vol. 3 of Theodor Storm, *Sämtliche Werke in vier Bänden*, ed. K. E. Laage and D. Lohmeier (Frankfurt, 1987/88), pp. 1051-82.

6 See: J. M. Ellis, 'Narration in Storm's *Der Schimmelreiter*', *The Germanic Review* 44 (1969), pp. 21-30, reprinted in J. M. Ellis, *Narration in the German Novelle* (Cambridge, 1974), pp. 155-68; M.G. Ward, *Theodor Storm: Der Schimmelreiter* (Glasgow Introductory Studies to German Literature 4, Glasgow, 1988); A. D. White, *Storm: Der Schimmelreiter* (Critical Guides to German Texts, London, 1988). W. Silz, 'Theodor Storm's *Schimmelreiter*', *Publications of the Modern Languages Association* 61 (1946), pp. 762-83, reprinted in his *Realism and Reality* (Chapel Hill, NC, 1954), pp. 117-37, is still worth looking at.

7 Cf. J. Hermand, 'Hauke Haien. Kritik oder Ideal des gründerzeitlichen Übermenschen', in his *Von Mainz nach Weimar 1793-1919* (Stuttgart, 1969), pp. 250-68; H. Segeberg, *Literarische Technik-Bilder, Studien zum Verhältnis von Technik- und Literatur-Geschichte im 19. und frühen 20. Jahrhundert* (Tübingen, 1987), pp. 55-106.

8 See Storm to Paul Heyse, 2 October 1884, in *Theodor Storm – Paul Heyse, Briefwechsel*, ed. C. A. Bernd, vol. 3 (Berlin, 1974), p. 94.

Classic European fiction published by Angel Books

THEODOR FONTANE
Effi Briest
Translated by Hugh Rorrison and Helen Chambers
Afterword and notes by Helen Chambers
0 946162 44 1 *(paperback)*

A new translation of Germany's best-loved nineteenth-century novel: a story of adultery in Bismarck's Prussia.
Shortlisted for the Weidenfeld Translation Prize 1996

'Fontane is a superb eavesdropper... the disarming casualness of narrative mode frequently reveals subtexts of extraordinary eloquence, even pathos... The translators have risen magnificently to the challenge.' – Martin Swales, *Times Higher Education Supplement*

'a new and superior English version of *Effi Briest*... accurate as no previous translation has been...' – David Sexton, *The Guardian*

THEODOR FONTANE
Cécile
Translated with an afterword and notes by Stanley Radcliffe
0 946162 42 5 *(cased)*   0 946162 43 3 *(paperback)*

The first English translation of the second of Fontane's 'Berlin' novels. At a fashionable spa in the Harz Mountains an affair develops between an itinerant civil engineer and the delicate, mysterious wife of a retired army officer. The dénouement is played out in the bustling capital of a newly unified Germany. Fontane was in love with his female characters 'for their human qualities, that is, for their weaknesses and sins.'

'*Cécile* is written with wit and a controlled fury and Radcliffe's elegant translation does it superb justice.' – Michael Ratcliffe, *The Observer*

Six German Romantic Tales
Translated with an introduction by Ronald Taylor
0 946162 17 4 *(paperback)*

Kleist's *Earthquake in Chile* and *The Betrothal on Santo Domingo*; Tieck's *Eckbert the Fair* and *The Runenberg*; Hoffmann's *Don Giovanni* and *The Jesuit Chapel in G.*

'All the varieties of the German Romantic movement are here: magical, political and aesthetic... Excellent translations.' – Stephen Plaice, *Times Literary Supplement*

HENRYK SIENKIEWICZ
Charcoal Sketches *and other tales*
Translated with an introduction and notes by Adam Zamoyski
0 946162 31 X (*cased*)   0 946162 32 8 (*paperback*)

Three novellas by the author of *Quo Vadis?* and *With Fire and Sword*. The title-story is a headlong satire on Polish village life under Tsarist rule. In *Bartek the Conqueror* a hero of the Franco-Prussian War finds he is no match for the Germans in the postwar peace. *On the Bright Shore* depicts a Polish expatriate community disporting itself on the French Riviera.

'Zamoyski's sprightly new translations demonstrate that the passage of a century cannot disguise the wit or lessen the bite of these three novellas.'
– *Publishers Weekly*

VSEVOLOD GARSHIN
From the Reminiscences of Private Ivanov *and other stories*
Translated with an introduction and notes by Peter Henry, Liv Tudge and others
0 946162 08 5 (*cased*)   0 946162 09 3 (*paperback*)

Garshin was the outstanding new writer in Russia between Dostoyevsky and Chekhov. His novellas and short tales include some of the best of Russian war stories, such as the epic title tale, and densely semiotic narratives like *The Red Flower* and *The Signal*. This selection, the most substantial in English for three quarters of a century, includes almost all Garshin's published fiction.

'Garshin's gift is an acute moral intelligence steadied by the economy of his style... It is legitimate to hear in the spare articulation of his prose the rhythm of Pushkin. This effect is well caught by Peter Henry and his colleagues.' – H. Gifford, *Times Literary Supplement*

ALEXANDER PUSHKIN
The Tales of Belkin *with* The History of the Village of Goryukhino
Translated by Gillon Aitken and David Budgen; introduction and notes by David Budgen
0 946162 05 0 (*paperback*)

Breathing the spirit of the Napoleonic era, *The Tales of Belkin* are among the most delightful stories in Russian literature. The linked *Village of Goryukhino* turns to Swiftian satire. The introduction and notes provide the fullest commentary in English on Pushkin's satirical range.

'twelve words in Russian: twelve in English. Pushkinian... exactitude and brevity.' – A.D.P. Briggs, *Times Higher Education Supplement*